Game in Diamonds

Game in Diamonds

by

Elizabeth Cadell

William Morrow and Company, Inc.

New York   1976

Printed in the United States of America.

1 2 3 4 5   80 79 78 77 76

Library of Congress Cataloging in Publication Data

Cadell, Elizabeth.
  Game in diamonds.
  I. Title.
PZ3. C11427Gam3   [PR9499.3.C3]   823'.9'12   75-34334
ISBN 0-688-03015-7

Book design by Arlene Goldberg

Chapter One

Mr. AINSTEY CLOSED the front door of his house, paused on the drive to sniff the freshness of the crisp May morning, and then set off at a brisk marching pace towards the road. He had a lean, upright figure, bushy grey hair, a heavy moustache and the carriage of a man full of confidence in himself. His expression, a mixture of arrogance and impatience, suggested that he held his fellow men in lower esteem.

He was on his way to call on a neighbour, but he was going in no friendly spirit. His mind was full of resentment—a pity, since it prevented him from noting the improvement in the weather. The sun, after weeks of absence, had returned and seemed to be seeking out old haunts. It had shone into the windows of Mr. Ainstey's house, skimmed over the peaceful hillside, filtered through the trees bordering the road and was now gleaming on the narrow, winding river along whose banks the town of Ellstream was spread. Beyond the river was the gently sloping hill on which stood a boys' preparatory school known as St. Godfric's. To east and west were farmhouses and stretches of market garden. The landscape seemed to breathe serenity.

It was this peaceful aspect that had made Mr. Ainstey decide, six years ago, to buy the site on which his house now stood. Only two plots had been offered for sale on the hillside along which he was walking; the higher slope had been retained by the owner and the rectangle below it divided into two plots differing greatly in size. The larger of these had been sold and was being built upon; only three acres remained.

Coming down from London on a visit of inspection, Mr. Ainstey had decided that Ellstream would be a perfect place for his approaching retirement. Situated in the heart of Somerset, it was a town very difficult to get to. The roads leading to it were narrow and winding. Only two trains a day ran in each direction, and the bus service was erratic. But these factors, which others might consider disadvantages, were welcomed by Mr. Ainstey, who had no intention of settling himself in a place to which friends and relations could flock with ease and frequency. The more deterrents, the better. He noted approvingly that the townspeople went about their business like the solid farming community that they were, displaying none of the tail-chasing activity that characterized so-called progressive towns. There was nothing to attract tourists. It was a place, he felt, in which he could build a modest house, get a good game of golf, join a bridge club and live in peace.

Two years later, he had retired, had built his house and had played golf and bridge. But the peace to which he had looked forward was missing.

He halted at the highest point of the road and turned to look down at the three houses built on the hillside. On three sides of them were woodland; the fourth side was open to the view of town and river. He could see the roof of his square, squat house, and part of its neat garden. He could also see the house to which he was making his way—a house with terraces and pillars and patios, a building he considered more suited to a Mediterranean setting than to the sober English countryside. Above both houses, its grounds spreading along their length, stood the mansion occupied by Lady Charlotte Merrion, widow of a rich banker.

Lady Charlotte had inherited the land on this hillside. Where her imposing house now stood, there had been for over two hundred years a deserted, crumbling ruin, flanked by a low, ugly brick tower. From time to time, attempts had been made by successive town councils to buy the land, but the owners had been hard to locate, and when located, proved apathetic and impossible to pin down to price. On hearing that she had inherited the property, Lady Charlotte came down from London, inspected it, reserved the upper half for herself and sold the rest. Her daughter-in-law, Mrs. Merrion, had bought the larger plot; Mr. Ainstey had bought the smaller.

Arriving in Ellstream after his retirement, bringing with him plans of the house he intended to build, he was very much annoyed to find that Mrs. Merrion had built a small guest cottage almost at the edge of his property. He rejected his architect's advice to place his own house farther away, for above and below the flat space he had chosen, the land sloped sharply, so that building would have been very much more expensive. When he had taken possession of his house, he realized that the money would have been better spent than saved, for it was the guest cottage that had wrecked his hopes of peace.

Gazing down at it now, he reviewed bitterly the countless occasions on which the guests in it had given him cause for complaint. Complaining, he found, had altered nothing. He was now on his way to inform Mrs. Merrion that after last night's disturbance, he had decided to cease protesting and have recourse to the law.

He strode on. A man had to take a firm line. Just before leaving his house that morning, he had taken a firm line on another matter. A request had been made to him by his sister-in-law and he had given an unhesitating and uncompromising refusal. No. Out of the question, he had said. Quite out of the question. There had been no argument; his sister-in-law, recognizing the finality in his tone, had simply gone into the kitchen and banged the door. He intended to apply the same firmness when dealing this morning with Mrs. Merrion. He had never before gone so far as to mention lawsuits, but she was going to hear something about them today. Protesting had been no use; he might just as well have saved his breath. She had always begun by pretending not to know what he was talking about. She had begged, very charmingly, to be enlightened. When he had enlightened her, she had looked distressed and promised earnestly to look into the matter—and then she had steered the conversation into other channels and offered him a drink and shelved the whole thing. She wouldn't find it so easy to shelve it today.

He reached the house, pushed open the gate and walked up the drive, forming in his mind the sentences with which he intended to launch his attack. He had borne enough. He would see to it that this time, he had her whole attention. This morning, she would have to listen.

Mrs. Merrion had been listening for some time. Seated in the small, sunny garden room that overlooked the town and the river, lying back on a chair which its makers claimed to follow the human form, her still-lovely legs stretched on the footrest, she had been listening to her son who, seated on a window seat, had put his request persuasively and at some length. When he ended, she spoke.

"No, Paul," she said. "I'm sorry, but I won't do it."

"Mother, you haven't been listening."

"Yes, I have. You want me to go to your wedding and come down the aisle after it clinging to your father's arm. Well, I won't. I've nothing against him. I've even exchanged polite conversation with him when we've run across one another, but I divorced him six years ago for good reasons and I'm not going to stage a sentimental scene coming down the aisle with him in the wake of you and your bride. He's been married to your stepmother— happily, you tell me—for over five years, so let her have his arm. I'll be with the rest of the guests."

Silence fell. She could not bring herself to believe that they were discussing his marriage. Why, she wondered, had the news, broken to her last night, found her so totally unprepared? Hadn't she always known that with his looks and his charm—*his?* No; *hers*—to say nothing of his money and his easy good nature and his generosity, he was a target for any woman aiming at a matrimonial prize? Paul Merrion, of Merrion's Bank. The only thing had been to hope that when he chose a wife, he would make a wise choice. Well, he hadn't. She did not know the girl he had chosen, but she knew her circle. She had known for the past few months that he was mixed up with the Framley set, but she had given him credit for more sense, more caution, more fastidiousness than to choose a wife from among its members.

He had given no hint of a possible engagement when he had telephoned from London three weeks ago asking if he could come and stay with her the last two weeks in May. He had said nothing about it when he drove up last night, dropped his suitcase in the hall and joined her in this room. She had welcomed him happily—it was not often, she pointed out, as he poured martinis for them both, that she had the privilege of his company for so long. Not a word of any personal matter had he spoken during dinner. Only as they sat drinking coffee afterwards did he break his news.

Having heard it, she had heard herself congratulating him, and she did not think that, well as he knew her, he had guessed at her disappointment and apprehension. The disappointment had diminished during the night, but the apprehension had sharpened. He had not looked, he had certainly not sounded happy. He had admitted that his intention had been to bring his fiancée with him on this visit, but his fiancée, instead of being with him, was with her mother in Venice. Something must be very badly wrong—but his manner did not invite enquiries. She remembered that she had often in the past complained that he was not serious enough; she could not complain now.

She broke the silence with a question.

"Does your father know?"

"No. I haven't seen much of him lately. He's been away—he and my stepmother went over to France—so I don't think he'll have heard any rumours. Did you tell Lottie I was coming?"

Nobody in the family, when speaking of her, ever referred to Lady Charlotte as anything but Lottie. When speaking to her, there was a marked increase of respect.

"Yes, I told her."

"Does she know the Framleys?"

"I've never heard her mention them."

"I don't suppose the news'll surprise her; she'll have had reports from all her spies in London."

"No, she hasn't."

"How do you know?"

"She was here yesterday morning, asking if you'd go and meet a guest who's coming to stay with her. A girl. She wouldn't have invited her if she'd had any suspicion you weren't free."

"Another wife for me, I suppose?"

"I imagine so."

"I wish to God she'd give up. She's been lining up candidates for years. Who's this latest one?"

"I don't know. But I know her uncle, and so do you— Professor Errol. He's coming too."

"Then why do I have to go and meet her?"

"They're not coming together. The Professor's coming from London. She's been staying with friends in Sussex. They're on their way to Scotland, where he's to lecture."

"How do they manage to get anybody to listen to him? You dragged me to one of his talks once—lethal, it was."

"Well, he's an authority on—"

"Oriental studies. I know. Why does his niece go with him? Is she an authority on Oriental studies too?"

"She acts as his secretary when he's lecturing. They're meeting at Lottie's and staying a few days and then they're going north together."

"This means that when I walk up this morning to tell Lottie I'm engaged, there won't be any congratulations."

"I don't think there will."

"Nice prospect." He spoke bitterly. "My fiancée in Venice, my grandmother about to work herself up into one of her rages—and a wedding with you sitting in a pew instead of trying to make the thing look like Happy Families."

She studied him for a while in silence. The dark looks of her Italian mother, passing her by, had settled on him. He could have passed unnoticed—except by women—on any street in Italy.

13

Her own fairness came from her father. He had been Ellstream's leading doctor and foremost citizen. A man of means, he had retired early and thereafter spent the winters in Italy. He had returned one spring with a beautiful Italian wife—like himself, middle-aged. Their only child, Antonia, had been born in the big, rambling riverside house—now a Nursing Home—which could be seen from the window seat on which Paul was sitting. She had lived in it until her marriage.

"You're not happy about my engagement, are you?" she heard Paul ask.

She hesitated. She could have pointed out that as far as outward appearances went, he himself could hardly have claimed to be happy. There was no sign of any return to his normal carefree manner; he was tense and irritable and—she thought—deeply worried.

"I don't know Diana Framley," she said. "But you told me last night that you'd planned to bring her down here to stay with me—in fact, that's why you took two weeks' leave. Isn't that right?"

"Yes."

"But instead of coming here, she changed her mind and went with her mother to Venice."

"The visit to Venice had been on the cards for some time. Mrs. Framley thought it would be a pity for Diana to miss it. Diana went because it was the last trip she and her mother would do together."

He admitted to himself that there were several inaccuracies in this statement. It was not the mother but the daughter who had made the decision to go to Venice. With the uninhibited frankness that characterized her, she had pointed out to Paul that a prince in Venice—if he could be persuaded to overcome his prejudice against matrimony—was a far bigger fish than a banker in Lon-

14

don. Her mother had pressed her to make a final attempt; she had decided to go, and Paul's protests had been met, as his protests had always been met, with laughter. He had let her go, first because he could not have prevented her, and second because this frankness of hers, this open, unabashed scheming, had from the beginning of their affair presented a challenge he had been forced to accept.

He turned and stared out at the view, but instead of hillside and river and town, he saw Diana Framley as he had first seen her. From the mists of memory emerged the lovely island of Jersey; he remembered his concentration on the task of adjusting the sails of his boat to round the entrance to the bay—and then he lifted his eyes and she was there, rushing towards him over the water, so swiftly that for a bewildering moment he had imagined she was flying. He recalled her beautiful, bronzed body, her dark hair whipped across her cheeks, the water skis on which she was balanced bounding on the waves as she went past him, her skill such that she could take him in at a glance and tell him by a curve of her lips that she found him pleasing. Sea, sun, speed and the perfection of a woman's body . . .

His mother spoke his name, and he turned.

"Where did you meet her?" she asked.

"Off the coast of Jersey. I was sailing. She was water-skiing."

She waited, but that seemed to be all.

"Don't be angry with me for not being more enthusiastic about your engagement," she pleaded. "It's just that I don't know and don't much like people like Mrs. Framley and her friends—and I don't understand how a girl, directly after becoming engaged, can leave her fiancé and go off somewhere with her mother. Nothing on earth could have got me away from your father just when we'd got engaged. And that's all I'm going to say about it." She paused. "There's an item of news I've got to tell you."

"Well?"

"Someone you know is staying in the guest cottage. I suppose you wouldn't care to guess who?"

"No. Tell me.

"Your uncle."

He stared at her in astonishment.

"Esmond? He's turned up again?"

"Yes."

"When?"

"Yesterday afternoon. I was on the point of telling you last night, but you began to tell me about your engagement, so Esmond went out of my head."

"You weren't crazy enough to invite him, were you?"

"Oh Paul, don't be silly. When did he ever wait for an invitation? He just arrived."

"Without luggage, as before?"

"He had a briefcase and a change of shirt and pyjamas—and I suppose a razor and a toothbrush."

"How long is it since he was last in England?"

"About three years."

"Did he give you any information as to how he'd spent them?"

"New South Wales, working on a farm. New Zealand, shearing sheep. On his way back to England, he says he took charge of skiing parties in Switzerland and then served in a beer garden in Austria. It could all be true, but probably isn't."

"How does he look?"

"Exactly the same. His hair's no greyer. He looks like your father's younger brother instead of his older brother."

"Did he go to see him?"

"Go to see your father? No."

"I needn't have asked. He's parked himself, as he did before, on the one member of the family who can't or won't see that he's a confirmed cadger. Even you must realize by now that he's past redemption—but you like him, don't you?"

"Like?" She considered. "In a way, yes. I know he's an awful liar, and I know he cadges and plays confidence tricks and he's even liable to pocket any ornaments people leave lying round—but somehow I can't make myself forget that he wasn't always like this. If his mother had had any understanding, any affection for him . . ."

"Odd, isn't it, how Father always got on with Lottie, and Esmond didn't?"

"Not really odd. Your father's the peace-loving type; he always gave in to her. Esmond wouldn't, and didn't, and so things got worse and worse until they had that awful row over his engagement, and he left England."

"Will anybody ever find out exactly how she managed to break it up?"

"I don't suppose so. He didn't even tell your father what happened."

"Be interesting to see if she tries to wreck my engagement. I suppose you've stacked the guest cottage with food and drink?"

"I put in enough for about a week. I've asked him to make his own meals in the cottage."

"Did you tell him I was coming?"

"Yes. He was delighted. He'll be along to see you some time this morning."

"If and when he comes, I'd rather you didn't mention my engagement."

She looked doubtful.

"He's bound to have heard of it from someone. He said he was in London for about a month before coming down here. He knows most of the people we know."

"How did he get here?"

"A man and his wife gave him a lift in their car—I met them for a few moments. I'm sorry in a way that he's here while you're here, but I don't suppose you mind. You like him as much as I do."

"I've never paid his bills and I've never lent him money."

"Well, don't begin. It's a tragedy, isn't it? All his looks and brains and personality—wasted. He would have made a good banker—better than your father, perhaps."

"Does Lottie know he's here?"

"She has a way of finding out things. But they'll keep out of each other's way, as they did when he was here before."

"What are you going to do when he runs out of supplies and starts running up bills in the town? Pay them, as you did last time?"

"I suppose so."

His eyes, resting on her, showed mingled affection and exasperation. There was a streak in her nature—he could not decide whether it was sentimental or superstitious—that made it impossible for her to refuse help to old friends who came to her with stories of hardship. This weakness—he counted it a weakness because the stories were almost invariably inventions—had led her to open her house and her purse to a succession of notably undeserving cases. The fact that she put them into the guest cottage did not lessen their nuisance value.

He had been wrong, he acknowledged, to imagine that after twenty-five years of busy social life in London, she would find Ellstream dull. Her return to the place in which she had been born had been wise; she had in this town roots deeper than he had realized, and she was essentially a countrywoman. She kept no resident servants; the cooking and the housework were done by women who came up daily from the town—daughters of those who had known or worked for her father. She did not often leave Ellstream; more and more, she had provided herself with pleasures and hobbies that kept her at home. The first had been the cultivation of water lilies, about which she had known nothing but about which she now knew as much as the enthusiasts who came long distances to see them. She bred and sold seal-point Siamese cats. Unable to decide between Great Danes and Alsatians, she had bought one of each. Her latest and most rewarding venture had been the purchase of several pairs of ornamental waterfowl; so fascinating had she found them that she bought several more pairs, had a large enclosure built and surrendered to them what had once been a swimming pool. Now only the ducks swam, providing a spectacle of grace and beauty seldom observed when guests had swum there.

He glanced out at the drive, and spoke without turning.

"Someone coming. Expecting anyone?"

"No. Do you recognize the car?"

"No car. Elderly guardsman type, marching in on his own feet."

She came to the window and gave an exclamation of annoyance.

"Who?" Paul enquired.

"Mr. Ainstey."

"Ainstey . . . Neighbours, aren't they?"

"Yes."

"Does he often drop in?"

"Never, except to complain."

"What about?"

"Oh . . . the guests in the cottage. Go and let him in, Paul."

Mr. Ainstey, entering, was met by her friendly greeting and a low growl from a Siamese cat occupying one of the chairs.

"How nice to see you. I don't think you've met my son. Paul, this is Mr. Ainstey, who lives next door."

"How do," Mr. Ainstey grunted. "Sorry to come unannounced, but—"

"Do sit down, won't you?"

"—but I've discovered," he continued, dispossessing the cat and taking its place, "that if I telephone in advance, you're always too busy to see me. So I took a chance on finding you in. I've come—best to speak out at once, and frankly—I've come, Mrs. Merrion, to tell you that something must be done about those guests you put into your cottage."

"Guests?"

Her tone was puzzled; she might have been wondering what guests were. Mr. Ainstey, not to be foiled by this familiar trick, turned to Paul.

"Not the first time I've come to tackle your mother on this subject," he told him. "If you think I'm howling before I'm hurt, let me put you into the picture. Before I built my house, I realized that your mother's guest cottage was rather too close to my property, but to build my own house further away would have meant extra expense which I felt I couldn't run to. While the building was going on, there was never any noise or disturbance from the guest cottage, so I decided I needn't put up a hedge or a fence; I simply planted a line of flowering shrubs. Now. There's no reason why your mother shouldn't put her guests a long way from her house; I'd do the same m'self, if I had guests. But nobody has any right to put a guest cottage on the fringe of a neighbour's property and then put into the cottage guests who make the kind of racket your mother's guests make. For four years, ever since I've been living here, I've had to put up with a lot of infernal noise. And not only noise. Noxious smells and—"

"Smells?" repeated Paul in surprise.

"Disgusting smells. Horrible. Curry, garlic and God only knows what other outlandish ingredients being cooked by the occupants.I have frequently been wakened by people singing late at night—singing or playing instruments. I have sometimes had to ask my wife to close all the windows. But last night was the climax. I will not have orgies taking place under my very eyes."

"Orgies?" Paul raised his eyebrows.

"Orgies? I don't understand," Mrs. Merrion said.

"I will explain. Last night, I was wakened by the sound of singing. I looked at my watch: midnight. I went to my window and looked out. There seemed to be a dozen or more people on the terrace in front of the cottage. They were in a circle, singing. In the middle of the circle was a woman, dancing. The moon was full and I could see quite clearly. She had no clothes on."

There was a pause.

"None?" enquired Mrs. Merrion at last.

"None whatever. Stark. And dancing. I think you must agree that a scene of that kind is not what one expects in a respectable neighbourhood. I don't think I exaggerate in calling it an orgy. I am glad to say that my wife is away; her window, like mine, opens on to the garden, and I am glad that she was not here to be a witness to proceedings of that kind almost in her own garden. I say 'almost', but there are actually footprints on my flower beds near the bushes. That, you know, is trespass. You can't expect—"

He stopped. At the low window had appeared the head

and shoulders of a man. He was clean-shaven, with grey hair worn long at the back. He was perhaps in his middle fifties; he was wearing a blue sports shirt that Paul recognized as one he had left here last summer. He spoke in a pleasant, cheerful voice.

"Good morning, Antonia. Hello, Paul—nice to see you again. You're looking very fit. Visitors?"

"Yes. You'd better come in, Esmond," Mrs. Merrion said.

Her brother-in-law swung a leg over the sill and stepped into the room.

"This is Mr. Ainstey, a neighbour," Mrs. Merrion told him. "He's here to complain about last night. Mr. Ainstey, this is my brother-in-law, Mr. Merrion."

"Saw him last night," Mr. Ainstey said without pleasure. "I am here," he told Esmond, "to explain that I will not tolerate any more inconvenience from the guests that Mrs. Merrion puts into her cottage. It stands at the edge of my garden, and from my bedroom window I can not only hear, but I can also see what is going on. Last night, I heard singing, and when I looked out, I saw a woman dancing. She was . . . she had nothing on. Nothing. She was—"

"Oh!" Esmond sounded like a man who had just seen the point of a rather involved story. He turned to Mrs. Merrion. "You met her, Antonia. Yesterday. She and her husband drove me down from London."

"Prancing, rather than dancing," Mr. Ainstey continued. "It was midnight, and the moon was full and—"

"That's why she was dancing," Esmond explained. "Midnight, and full moon—and mild. It was one of the most perfect nights I've ever seen. I could have danced myself. I don't say I would have removed my clothes, but that's only because I'm not young and I'm not beautifully made. Her figure—as you saw—is one of Nature's masterpieces. And dancing, incidentally, is her profession. What you saw, lucky fellow, was a preview of a dance she's going to do in her next show. A preview and a free view."

"I did not want either. The whole scene, to my mind, was disgraceful."

"Oh, my dear fellow"—Esmond spoke in amused protest—"you mustn't make it sound like an orgy. Let's forget it and drink to the success of the show. Antonia, may I ask Paul to act as bar boy?"

"I will not drink anything, thank you," Mr. Ainstey said. "I came to—"

"Are you," Esmond broke in, "by any chance one of the Lincolnshire Ainsteys? If so, you must be related to Lord Gillingly. I was talking to him the other day, and I'll be seeing him again soon—may I convey a message?"

If anybody else had made that remark, Paul reflected, it would have sounded exactly what it was: a too-obvious attempt at a diversion. But Esmond's success as a con man was based on his acting ability, and Mr. Ainstey, staring at him suspiciously, encountered in his gaze nothing but warm interest and expectancy.

"Afraid not," It was hard to disown a peer, but facts were facts. "I'm from Gloucestershire."

"Ah. The Fitzroy Ainsteys. I know them well. Their grandson's coming on splendidly in cricket, isn't he? You must be jolly proud of him. I shouldn't be surprised if he got his cap this year. Sherry, Antonia?"

"No, thanks. It's a bit early for me."

"Then Paul and I will drink together." He raised his glass. "To our better acquaintance," he told Mr. Ainstey. "I shall see to it that no more of my friends disturb your rest, and I proffer a deep apology. What happened, Antonia, was that after leaving me at the cottage, they went down and dined in the town and got into conversation with some amusing people and brought them up to the cottage. I was foolish enough to offer them a drink. I should have sent them away. You know, Mr. Ainstey, I can see part of your garden from the cottage windows—I like that charming sundial you've got in the center of the lawn."

A flush of gratification showed on Mr. Ainstey's cheeks.

"Made it m'self. Going to put a base round it soon. A kind of brick surround. Give it a nice finish." He paused, coughed, looked as though he was trying to remember what he came for, and then took his leave.

"Sorry to have raised the point," he mumbled to Mrs. Merrion, "but I'd like to feel that in future—"

"You may rely on me," Mrs. Merrion promised. "Paul, will you see Mr. Ainstey out?"

Mr. Ainstey, after having had his hand warmly shaken by Esmond, walked with Paul into the hall.

"Staying long?" he asked.

"About two weeks."

"I don't think I've ever seen you down here before."

"I come fairly frequently, but only for a day or two. My mother's hard to move nowadays; she thinks a journey up to London's something of an expedition." He opened the front door. "Pity in a way that the guest cottage isn't at the end of my grandmother's estate. She wouldn't have been as long-suffering as you appear to have been."

This unexpected, obviously sincere tribute, coming so soon after he had been linked with a peer and grafted on to a prominent county family, melted the last of Mr. Ainstey's resentment. He fixed keen eyes on Paul, and liked what he saw. Their leave-taking was cordial. And at that moment there was born in Mr. Ainstey's mind an idea that struck him as so brilliant, so full of possibilities, that he walked homeward in a daze. Two birds with one stone, he muttered to himself as he went. If it didn't work, nobody would ever know that he had had anything to do with it. If it worked, there it was: two birds with one stone . . .

Paul began to close the door, and then changed his mind. He had to pay a visit to his grandmother. It was the last thing in the world he wanted to do, but it had to be done, and there was no point in postponing it. He stepped onto the drive and closed the door behind him.

On his way to her house, he tried to answer the question his mother had been unable to answer: did his grandmother know the Framleys? He thought it probable; she had not, like his mother, removed all her interests from London to Ellstream. She went frequently to the flat she still owned in Pont Street, and she had during her long widowhood kept in touch not only with her own friends, but also with those of her late husband. She did not often pay visits, but guests came frequently to her house at Ellstream.

That she had so many friends was something which had never ceased to puzzle Paul. Nobody, he mused, taking the short cut through the woods, could call her an agreeable woman. She was without a vestige of humor; she could be blunt to the point of insult; she held strong and prejudiced views on politics, sex and society and had never been known to change them. Cold and reserved by nature, very little of her character appeared on the surface. One had to be a member of her family to have witnessed or been subjected to one of her rages.

She was not liked in Ellstream, but she was respected —or more accurately, valued by those to whom she brought benefits. The town planners were grateful to her because she had pulled down the ruin that had stared sightlessly down at the town for so long, and replaced it by a handsome mansion. The committees of those local charities she approved of had reason to thank her for generous donations. The tradespeople were grateful because she bought all her stores locally, ran up large bills and paid them regularly, thus compensating for the fact that delivery vans made almost as many journeys up the hill to take back the goods she found unsatisfactory, as they made to deliver goods she had ordered. Her servants—a Goanese family of mother, father and two daughters—had been in her service for over twenty years.

It was an extremely handsome house, Paul acknowledged as he came in sight of it. Everything had been done as she always did everything—with impeccable taste and without regard to expense. Those who knew her were not surprised at her building, at her advanced age, a house so little in keeping with the times, but she had been born and reared in elegance and spaciousness, and her money had enabled her to recreate these conditions wherever she had lived.

He paused midway down the long approach to the house. Here the drive widened, narrowing again a little farther on. In the center of the wide circle stood the only object which his grandmother had retained from the two-hundred-year-old ruin: a small, graceful bronze statue of Hermes, about two feet high, standing on a low stone plinth. It had not been moved; the drive had been constructed round it, and the front door of the house placed in a direct line with it, giving unusual interest to the approach.

He walked on, missing as he drew nearer the greeting that dogs gave him when he approached his mother's house. His grandmother did not like animals, so there were no friendly or warning barks, no wagging tails or bared teeth.

He rang. The door was opened by Joseph, the butler, the darkness of his skin accentuated by his spotless linen. Yes, her ladyship was in.

Paul was shown into the small, in summer rather stuffy room opening off the dining room; shown in because he had learned better than to bypass Joseph and find his own way. Informality was not encouraged. His grandmother was writing letters at a desk; she turned, nodded, put down her pen and unsmilingly inclined her cheek for his kiss. Then she rose and led him to the two armchairs near the window. She did not move, he thought, like a woman close to her eightieth birthday; her movements, though slow, were not stiff. He wondered, as he had wondered since boyhood, how a woman who looked so mild could be so formidable. There was nothing about her appearance that gave strangers the slightest hint of her dictatorial tendencies. She was neither tall nor imposing; she was small and thin. Her voice was soft, its tone mild. The style of her dress was outmoded, but its quality and cut perfect. Her hair, which he knew to be a wig, was a neat arrangement of soft grey waves.

"Sit down," she invited. "How is your mother?"

She had seen his mother the day before. But with his grandmother, no preliminaries were ever skipped.

"She's very well, thank you."

"And you?"

"I'm fine, thanks, Gran."

"You came down from London by car?"

"Yes."

"The car you were driving when I saw you last?"

"No. This is another one. How is yours behaving?"

"It's very comfortable. I'm told I don't use it enough. I have a new chauffeur—you know my last one went back to India?"

"Yes, I heard. What's the new one like?"

"He seems satisfactory. He's Joseph's nephew."

This was no surprise to Paul; he knew that Joseph produced extra members of staff whenever they were needed, seemingly out of a hat. He would have liked to know how he managed it, but had never ventured to enquire.

"Has your father," his grandmother asked him, "said anything to you about this idea he has of retiring?"

"He mentioned it, but I didn't think he was serious. Anyway, he's still appearing regularly and he's still running things."

"I called it his idea. I was wrong. His wife is at the back of it."

The two words—his wife—spoken in that tone would have informed any listener of Lady Charlotte's feelings. Her younger son's divorce had been something against which she had fought bitterly and, when defeated, never forgiven. She was aware that the strength to withstand her had not come from him. Paul, up to that time, had been uncertain what her feelings were towards his mother; there had never been any outward show of affection or even approbation. But the fact that she had so strongly opposed the divorce had been one sign of liking, and there had soon been another: when she had come unexpectedly into possession of the land in Ellstream, she had displayed not the slightest interest in the fact that her daughter-in-law had been born and brought up in the town. But once divorce proceedings were instituted, she decided to build a house on the hill, and she had used every inducement to persuade her daughter-in-law to buy the large plot below it and build a house on it.

"I don't think," he answered his grandmother, "that my stepmother had much to do with it. She's never shown much interest in the Bank."

"She wants to travel. That's to say, she wants to drift from one expensive resort to another, dressed in little more than bare skin. She has the figure for it. She wants your father to escort her now, while he's comparatively young; she doesn't want to have to tow him. So she's persuading him to retire. I daresay you'll make as good a banker when your time comes to take over."

"I hope so." Paul, to his annoyance, heard himself clearing his throat nervously. "Gran, there's some news I—"

"That your uncle has turned up again?"

"Well, no. I mean, yes, he has, but it wasn't that that I—"

"Then you're going to tell me you're engaged?"

"Yes. How did you . . . I mean, you've heard?"

"I'm not exactly buried alive, you know. I have friends in London. They write to me. Several of them mentioned your inexplicable liking for the society of the Framleys, but I preferred to ignore rumours. You now tell me you're engaged?"

"Yes, I am."

"I've seen no announcement."

"There hasn't been one."

"Why not?"

"We didn't think it necessary to rush into print at once."

"It's usual. With a woman like Mrs. Framley, it's routine. You do realize, I suppose, that old-fashioned people like myself—people with standards—wouldn't dream of having anything to do with people like the Framleys? I—"

"I know that—"

"Kindly allow me to finish. I, and your mother after me, were the wives of prominent men. There were few people of any consequence in London who were not on our visiting list. We entertained constantly and, on ceremonial occasions, lavishly. But we made certain rules about certain people—people like the Framleys. We did not judge; we did not discuss them or condemn them; we merely avoided them. You would have done well to do

29

the same. A wealthy young man like yourself has to exercise more care than those less privileged when it comes to choosing friends and associates. Nobody ever interfered with your pleasures, because we felt, as a family, that you had a level head—to say nothing of a sense of responsibility."

Her tone had not changed; as so often before, he was hearing harsh words spoken with so little emphasis, so little heat, that he could scarcely believe they were being uttered. There was a pause, and then the mild voice went on.

"I wouldn't dwell on these facts if I thought that you were going to marry this girl, but I don't think you are."

He fought a desire to push back his chair and walk out of the room, and managed to speak calmly.

"What do you think is going to get in the way? Are you suggesting that—"

"Mrs. Framley is going to get in the way."

"Mrs. Framley has given her consent to—"

"Quite so."

"And now you want me to believe that she's going to try and stop me from—"

"It isn't a matter of stopping you. What she's going to do—what she has in fact already done—is prevent you from starting. If, as you state, you've just become engaged to her daughter, why has she taken her abroad for an indefinite period?"

"Not indefinite. A matter of two or three weeks. She thought that the announcement could wait until she—they—got back from Venice. She thought it would be a pity for Diana to miss the trip."

"And so it would have been. Venice in May is very pleasant, and they're staying, I'm told, in a palazzo belonging to one of those playboy princes."

"They're old friends."

"I daresay. Birds of a feather. Debauchery, drunkenness and drugs. Those would be your friends, if you married Miss Framley. I'm happy to think that you won't get a chance to do so."

"Listen to me, please. I—"

"No. You listen to me. You're thirty-two years old, healthy, well-educated and you've got a good deal of money. That adds up to a total that would satisfy most girls and most mothers. The only prospect better than yourself is a man with a title—and that's what Mrs. Framley and her daughter have gone after in Venice. The idea of letting you imagine yourself engaged was simply to keep you in storage for a time while they had a last ambitious dip in the matrimonial pool. I would have thought that a man with even an elementary knowledge of the world would have learned to keep away from ti-gresses like the Framleys. But I oughtn't to be surprised. How many girls of good background, girls who would have made excellent wives, have I found for you during the past ten years?"

"I didn't count."

"Eight. And you showed not the slightest interest in any of them. Well, engaged or not, you happen to be free at the moment, so I hope you'll be civil to a girl I've invited to stay with me. She's arriving the day after to-morrow, and as the only other people in the house will be myself and her uncle, who's far from young, she's going to find things a little dull. I would like you to go and meet her—she arrives on the morning train. I can't send my car, because it's going to London to fetch her uncle. It'll give you something to do. There's no point in your mooning about wishing you were in Venice. If you were wanted in Venice, it must be clear even to you that they wouldn't have left you behind. This girl's name is Yolanda Purvis. She's interested in horses; in fact, she trains them, so you might arrange some riding for her. I shall of course reimburse you for any expenses you incur on her behalf. I would like you and your mother to dine here on the evening of their arrival. I hope your mother will ask them to lunch or dinner while they're here; it'll only be about a week, so I don't feel it's asking too much, either of you or of her. And now will you leave me to finish my letters?"

She rose. Once more the soft, smooth cheek was offered. She had pressed a bell. Joseph came in, Paul was shown out. He went without a word, heard the front door close behind him and stood still to take in air. She had done it again, he told himself in fury. Poison, gently administered. Everything she wanted to say, said. Straight to the point. No skirting the topic, no extraneous remarks or enquiries, no interest shown in his mother's reactions to his engagement, no dwelling on the fact that his uncle was back again. No opportunity for the victim to break in and say a word or two.

He walked slowly homeward, his mind full of bitterness. If he had been able to say anything, what would he have said? Only that he had fallen in love. But nobody was interested in anything but the scandalous Framley record—and he had known the Framley record long before he asked Diana Framley to marry him. He had known; it would not be true to say, even to himself, that he had not cared. He had cared a great deal, but he had backed himself against her past. At the moment it looked as though he had made a bad bet. He hadn't been able to keep her from going to Venice; was it likely that he would be able to prevent her from doing anything, however outrageous, she chose to do in the future?

He let his mind range over the past few months. He had not, he knew, been happy—but he had told himself that he had been something more: intensely alive, responsive, alert. He had been on guard, his nerves and senses stretched, moving in a world in which he had known himself to be an outsider. He could match the other men she knew in physique and finance; what she missed in him, he realized, was that extra quality which those men had which matched her own recklessness. There had been, during his association with her, no moment of boredom; she, and those about her, took the sweets from life's table and left the rest. There were no problems, because problems were for tomorrow, and perhaps tomorrow would never come. There was no future shadow, even for her ageless mother. There had been movement, a breathtaking pace, stimulation and a kind of satisfaction.

But there had never been the element he was facing now. There had never been any hint of humiliation. He could not bring himself to believe that they had put him on a shelf and would leave him there until the time came—if it came—to take him down again. His mother, his grandmother, his other relations and those who had once been his friends could see him dangling, waiting. If he went to Venice, he would be breaking the agreement. She was promised to him, but there had been a proviso. He had been warned. If she failed to come back to him, he could not—she had said—complain.

He found his mother in the garden, walking aimlessly. He joined her without speaking, and they turned towards the house.

"I've seen Lottie," he said after a time. "I thought I'd better get it over."

"Did she know?"

"Yes. She said it wouldn't come off. She said Mrs. Framley would see to that. She said that in fact, Mrs. Framley already had. Is that what you think too?"

She hesitated.

"I've been wondering," she said at last. "If you don't mind my saying so, the signs aren't hopeful. It's not the mother I'm thinking of; it's the girl. If she could go away now . . ."

"She makes her own rules."

"I suppose she does." She stopped at the wire of the waterfowl enclosure and stared unseeingly at a pair of newly arrived mandarins. "I feel I'm not really competent to judge. I've met people like the Framleys—who hasn't?—but when that happened, they thought me terribly boring and dull, and I thought they were unreal, artificial. I don't see how a girl from a set, a setting like that could make you a good wife and bring up your children in the way you were brought up—for what that's worth. But if you say it's all right, I'll believe you."

There was silence. The mandarins flew over the pool and settled on the grass beyond. She wondered if either of them had ever had any doubts as to the faithfulness of its mate.

She heard Paul speaking quietly.

"I can't remember," he said, "when she first mentioned Venice. I thought, when she did, that she was speaking in the past tense, talking about the Italian who'd come to London last autumn. She began vaguely, but it was clear enough in the end. I realized she wasn't speaking in the past, but in the future. She wasn't talking about the visit he'd made in autumn; she was telling me about the visit she and her mother were going to pay now. She asked for comments, but I knew and she knew that nothing I said would make any difference to her plans. What she wanted to do, she'd do. Wherever she chose to go, she'd go—with me, or without me."

He paused; she said nothing. After a while, he continued in the same tone.

"I knew, when I met her, exactly what I was getting into. She thought most of my ideas archaic—farcical. I had to readjust. For example, I'd thought of myself as a widely travelled man, but she didn't know the meaning of distance. She'd take off at a day's notice for India or Istanbul or Peru or Patagonia, and be back almost as soon as she went. Expense never acted as a check. If her friends wanted to see her, she felt they ought to be—and they always were—prepared to pay her expenses. She knew what a prize she was—how could she help knowing? Beautiful body, a beautiful nun's face, elegance, vitality. She was a prize, and men had to compete for the prize. Men did. I wasn't the first who'd won it, but I was certain, for a time I was absolutely certain that I'd be the last. And now she's in Venice, and I agreed to wait, and I thought I'd be content to wait—but I'm not. Since leaving, she hasn't been in touch. I've heard nothing from her—she hasn't written and she hasn't rung up." He turned to look at her, and the misery on his face made her tremble. "So what do I do? Am I crazy to stay here mooning, as Lottie calls it? I agreed to wait—but now I'm wondering what I'm waiting for. And I'm wondering whether it's worth waiting for."

Again, she said nothing; there seemed nothing to say.

"I made a mistake," he went on after a time, "in suggesting bringing her down here to meet you. I said I wanted you two to get to know one another. She said I sounded like one of my clerks. I think it was then that she began to have doubts about marrying me. She'd been certain that I was ... integrated, but this proposal to bring her here made her realize that there was still a wide gap between us. She was afraid that I was trying to cut her out of the herd, separate her from her set. She was right."

They went into the house, and Paul opened the door of the garden room.

"A drink," he said. "We both need it." He poured drinks and brought her her glass. "If I've worried you, I'm sorry. But at the same time, I'm glad I've told you how

35

things stand. To return to Lottie: she knew Esmond was here."

"Did she mention this girl she invited?"

"Yes. Name of Yolanda Purvis. Horsey. Arriving the day after tomorrow on the morning train, and I'm to go and meet her. And you're to invite her to lunch or dinner, or both, and I'm to take her out, passing the bills on to Lottie. And you and I are to go up and dine with her on the evening of their arrival. A full and exciting programme, don't you agree?" He gave a bitter smile. "You can see, can't you, that bringing Diana Framley down here wouldn't exactly have fitted in with her idea of fun?"

Chapter
Two

MR. AINSTEY, NEARING HIS HOUSE, was wrestling with the details of the scheme which had sprung into his mind on Mrs. Merrion's doorstep. Totally unaccustomed to dealing with original ideas, he decided to make a detour through the woods in order to give himself time to think.

He had never in his life acted on impulse; his method was to plan and ponder and—perhaps—to perform. A man of narrow interests, he had spent his working life at a desk in a tea importer's office in the City; his hobby, and his pride, had been to keep himself fit. He had few friends; of these, none was very close. Women he sedulously avoided. He was close on sixty when he decided to marry.

When he met his wife, she had been Eunice Cresset, a widow with four young daughters. She and her first husband had lived in London, in a large, out-of-date house which belonged to her brother, who had made his home in New Zealand, and who, when she was widowed, allowed her to go on living in the house at a moderate rent—an acknowledgement of his realization that she was going to find it hard to make ends meet. She had no money and no training for any kind of profession. Her eldest daughter was fourteen, the youngest eight.

The house was a cold, rambling one, but it suited her; it backed on to gardens and it was near a good day school. It also had a suite of rooms on the ground floor in which she decided to put paying guests. Her only gifts—almost her only interests—were cooking and housekeeping, and she knew that she could make her guests comfortable.

The scheme received strong support from her sister, Brenda, who had left her husband after one of the shortest spells of married life ever recorded, and was working in an office in York. Brenda came to London, joined Eunice and became a useful and enlivening member of the household. Unlike the quiet, somewhat colourless Eunice, she had a shrewd, clear-seeing mind and an irrepressible sense of humour. She also had a tongue that could scorch.

Mr. Ainstey had been the first paying guest—and the last. Calling at the house in answer to Mrs. Cresset's advertisement, he inspected the rooms, haggled over their price, stated that he would require all three and then announced that he would come on a month's trial, his tone making it clear that the trial would be made on his side only. At the end of the month, he expressed himself satisfied and asked that the rooms be cleared of furniture to make room for his own. He then settled down and for the next ten years enjoyed a standard of comfort superior to anything he had ever known.

At the end of this period, several events combined to bring the arrangement to an end. The first was that Mrs. Cresset's brother died, and his widow, not unnaturally anxious to profit by the steep rise in London property values, announced her intention of selling the house. Next, Brenda fell ill, and the doctors held out very little hope of her recovery. And finally, Mrs. Cresset's three eldest daughters left London to fill teaching posts in the provinces.

At this juncture, Mr. Ainstey, with the stiffness and formality which made him so unpopular with the young, offered himself to Mrs. Cresset. He was, he told her, on the point of retiring; he was building a house on a plot of land in Somerset; as his wife, she would have a free hand in furnishing and embellishing it. He would do his best to make her happy.

When Mrs. Cresset, to his surprise and chagrin, hesitated, he decided to go further; he would, he promised, give each of the four girls a reasonable allowance, to be discontinued when they married. To clinch matters, he used Brenda, whom he detested, as bait: he offered her a home, so that her sister could nurse her for the brief remaining period of her life.

No man had ever been more contented than Mr. Ainstey as he installed his mature bride in her new house. Nothing had been said between them of love, or even of affection, but they had grown to know one another well, and knew that there were no surprises in store. If it was less a marriage than a business arrangement, there was between them respect and, on her side, a strong sense of duty. Both had gained what they most wanted. She, the home lover, had a house to run and someone to cook for. He, the comfort-lover, congratulated himself on capturing a woman who belonged to that almost-extinct species: one who knew how to minister to a man. Settling in, he overcame his distaste for household tasks long enough to hang some pictures and lay a carpet. Once or twice he was even seen carrying a glass of Madeira to Brenda as she lay, pale and listless, on a long chair in the garden, her gaze on the peaceful hillside.

Then Providence, hitherto so cooperative, dealt Mr. Ainstey a severe blow. Brenda did not die. Breathing the unpolluted, invigorating air of Ellstream, she began to revive. Worse, in Mr. Ainstey's view, she went on reviving. But by the time she had fully recovered, he had made the discovery that the term labour-saving, applied to housework, did not mean all that he had taken it to mean. In spite of the modern equipment he had installed, there was still a great deal more labour than his wife could accomplish alone. The numerous women down in the town, said by the architect to be eagerly awaiting a summons to come and work, had been summoned and had failed to appear. The only help at hand was Brenda, and Mr. Ainstey was faced with the choice of allowing her to occupy in his house the post of unpaid domestic assistant which she had held in London—or letting her go, and becoming an unpaid domestic assistant himself. He made his choice: Brenda stayed. As in London, she kept out of his way. She occupied the small room and bathroom which had been intended for guests, arranged the kitchen in the form of a miniature snack bar, and there took her meals alone. She retired to her room after dinner. She missed her nieces, but their absence gave her a certain amount of leisure which she used to organize and direct in Ellstream a band of about thirty volunteers who, calling themselves The Extra Hands, took turns at giving service to the lonely and the aged.

The household settled down, and Mr. Ainstey found that he had guessed right in thinking that the allowances he paid to his stepdaughters would not long be a charge on his purse. The three eldest married; there remained only the youngest, and as she was also the prettiest, he had no doubt that she, like her sisters, would soon be snapped up. He looked forward to seeing the last of her—and he was not thinking only of his purse; he had found her, from her childhood, a source of intense irritation. In the house in London, she had shown him none of the deference which her better-behaved sisters had done. Far from heeding his demands for silence, she had daily capered noisily down the stairs, stampeded through the hall and banged the front door. She had refused to confine her violin practice to the hours in which he was out of the house. Whenever he expostulated, she gazed up at him with an exaggerated, wide-eyed awe that was infinitely more galling than insolence. More than anything else, her name—Lydia—irritated him. At the age of fourteen, he had been shamelessly pursued by a sixteen-year-old Lydia. His panic had long since subsided, but the name had remained in his mind as a symbol of unbridled sex. Why couldn't she have been given a homely name, like her sisters Susan and Kathleen and Dorothy? The sooner she found herself a husband and removed herself, as they had done, to places too far away to allow frequent visits to Ellstream, the happier he would be.

But she was now twenty-two, an age at which her sisters had been engaged or married, and she was still single, still unattached and still drawing the allowance he paid her, acknowledging it only by a line scrawled inside a Christmas card. Unlike her outstandingly clever sisters, she had shown no academic prowess; her school reports had been tantamount to successive sighs of despair. He did not think her skill as a violinist could be as great as her mother imagined, for on leaving the music college at which she had studied, she had tried and failed to get into a national orchestra, and had finally joined a group known as the Kellerman String Quartet. He did not follow the quartet's fortunes, but he noted that most of their engagements were in small and unregarded towns, and went unnoticed by the critics. And it was all very well for her mother to say that several men were anxious to marry her; he would believe it when he saw her at the altar or in the registry office. He had almost come to believe that she was remaining single in order to spite him.

But this morning, returning from his visit to Mrs.

Merrion, he felt that at last he could do something to get her off his hands. He would do it by giving her an opportunity which it would be madness for her to miss. There, next door, staying with his mother and looking as though he was finding it very dull, was a young man who must surely appeal to any girl, even one as selective as his stepdaughter appeared to be. Here was a man single, good looking if you cared for that dark type, the son of Merrion of Merrion's Bank. The only son. All that was required was to get her up here and leave the rest to Nature.

Getting her up here, unfortunately, involved going back on what he had said to his sister-in-law before leaving the house that morning. But he'd do it at once, and close his ears to any sardonic comments she cared to make.

When he let himself into his house, the sound of the vacuum cleaner led him to his study, a small room opening off the hall. He had deeply resented moving out of it in order to accommodate his stepdaughters when they came on visits, and he had flatly refused to move out for their husbands; this attitude had resulted in an arrangement that his wife would in future do the visiting. Accordingly, she set out each spring, leaving Brenda to run the house, and went on a round of visits to her four daughters. She had chosen, this year, to go away in May, and she had been gone for two weeks.

That morning, Brenda had stopped Mr. Ainstey as he was leaving the house. In her brusque manner, she told him that she had a request to make. This, to his astonishment, proved to be a suggestion that Lydia should come on a visit.

"Lydia?" he repeated. "What for? She's only just seen her mother. What do you want her here for?"

"To give her a holiday. She hasn't had one this year.

She didn't have one last year, either. She's not working at the moment; one of the members of the quartet left and they're waiting to get a fourth. It isn't often she gets enough spare time to take a holiday. It's bad enough to live in a semi-basement room in a boarding house in Pimlico. To live in it without ever getting a holiday is a good deal worse."

She had very little hope that he would agree to the visit. Lydia had received so cold a welcome two years ago that she had had no wish to repeat the visit.

"Do you expect me," demanded Mr. Ainstey, "to give up my study for her?"

"No, I don't. Her mother's room is free; why can't she use it?"

"Out of the question. And may I remind you how much the telephone bill amounted to last time she came here? It never stopped ringing—except when she was using it to ring up her friends. The bill for that quarter was—"

"I know what it was. You told me. You told me two years ago and you've been telling me ever since. Well, that's all. Thank you for nothing."

She had gone into the kitchen, banged the door behind her and left him to add up all the things about her that he disliked. She was the antithesis of her sister in most things—but in appearance, they could have been identical twins, and this uncanny physical resemblance never failed to disconcert him. It was as though his wife sometimes fell under an evil spell, uttering curt, abrupt sentences and looking at him as though he belonged to a rare zoological species.

Yes, he would have to eat his words, the words he had spoken before he went out. She wouldn't make it easy for him.

She was working with her back to the door, and the sound of the vacuum cleaner prevented her from hearing

43

his entrance or his opening words. He went forward and switched it off, and she turned to face him.

"What did you do that for?" she demanded.

"I want to talk to you."

"I'm busy. Can't it wait?"

"No. I've been thinking over what I said to you this morning."

"So have I. What are you going to do—say it all over again?"

"I've decided that there was something in your idea, after all."

"What idea?"

"The idea of asking Lydia down here for a holiday."

He waited. She said nothing; she merely looked at him with her eyebrows raised.

"I wanted time," he lied, "to consider your suggestion of putting her into her mother's room."

"Well, you've had time. Two hours all but twenty minutes."

"I've decided that it would be quite a good idea."

"What would?"

"To use Eunice's room."

"Use it for what?"

"The suggestion came from you. If you remember, I asked whether you expected me to turn out of my study, and you—"

"I said no, I didn't expect."

He went on doggedly, fighting a longing to throw a heavy book at her.

"I think you need some help in the house. You're not getting any younger and—"

"I'm only two hours minus twenty-one minutes older."

"—and I think it would be a good thing if Lydia came and gave you a hand with the work while Eunice is away."

As soon as he had spoken the words, he realized that he had made a mistake. He knew, she knew, everybody who knew Lydia knew that her skill at cooking barely ran to boiling eggs, while her housekeeping method was to let the work pile up for as long as possible, and then make an assault on the accumulation. He was not surprised to see Brenda staring at him as though he had deprived her of speech.

"Lydia—give me a hand with the work?"

"Yes. There's a lot to do, and Eunice isn't here to help you."

"She hasn't been here for the past two weeks to help me."

His self-control left him.

"Did you, or did you not suggest bringing her up here?" he shouted.

"Don't bawl at me. Yes, I made the suggestion. And you turned it down. You said no."

"Well, I've changed my mind."

"Why?"

"Because I've had time to think, that's why. You stop a man just as he's going out of the house, you throw a suggestion to him and expect him to give an instant reply. You know very well that I like to have time to mull over proposals before agreeing to them."

"Well, you've mulled. And if I ask her, you'll mull again and say she isn't to come after all."

"My mind is made up. I shall not change it again. Put a call through to her this evening."

"You mean . . . *phone* her?"

"Do you think I meant you to use a megaphone?"

"You gave orders, strict orders that no phoning was to be done if writing could be done instead."

"I meant, simply, that telephoning can become a habit. An expensive habit. Half the calls could just as well—"

"I'm to telephone to Lydia and tell her that you're inviting her to come and stay?"

"Put it any way you please. That's up to you. But do it."

He walked out of the room, and she stared after him with speculation in her eyes. The idea of helping her with the work she dismissed as pure smoke screen. What had made him go back on . . .

There was nothing to be gained, she decided, in trying to guess his reason. He had stated clearly that Lydia was to come; that was enough. There might be a clash or two while she was here, but at least she would be out of that dreary little room, breathing some healthy country air.

She put a call through when Mr. Ainstey went out to weed the garden. There was no reply. She tried again when he was at dinner—no reply. When he went up to bed, she tried again, and this time heard the voice of Lydia's landlady, Mrs. Lyle.

"Yes, who's that?"

"May I speak to Miss Cresset, please?"

"Miss who did you say?"

"Cresset. *C-r-*"

"Oh, Cresset. Hang on a mo, will you? I'll find out if she's in."

There was a pause during which Brenda heard the tinkle of the handbell that hung on a string over the banisters and was rung to summon the basement dwellers to the telephone. After an interval, she heard Lydia's voice.

"Who is it?"

"Brenda."

"Oh. There's nothing wrong, is there?"

"Why should anything be wrong?"

"You told me phoning was strictly forbidden. You're supposed to write."

46

"Not this time. Did you find somewhere for your mother to stay?"

"Yes. Just next door. Nice room and bath. But she's not in London anymore; I put her on the train for Carlisle days ago. Did you want to get hold of her?"

"No. What I'm ringing for is to ask if you can come down for a week or two."

"Come down?"

"Yes."

"Come down where?"

"Don't be silly. Here, of course."

"You mean you're inviting me to Ellstream?"

"Yes."

"Why? Is he away?"

Mr. Ainstey's first name was George, but neither Brenda nor Lydia ever used it; they used the pronoun.

"No, he isn't away. He's here."

"Then what on earth's got into you? Don't you remember how awful it was two years ago? If I appeared, he'd probably drop dead. Is that why you're asking me?"

"I'm asking you because—"

"It must be pretty awful to be stuck up there all alone with him, but with me there, it'd be a lot worse. Is he being worse than usual?"

"No. Will you listen instead of talking? You wrote and said that your quartet had—"

"—shrunk. That's right. We're down to three. The leader skipped, taking a girl friend and the cash box. So we're waiting to—"

"Will you listen? You're free, aren't you?"

"For the moment, yes."

"Well then, you can come here. He told me to ask you. He— What's so funny?"

"Nothing. I thought for a moment you said he'd asked me."

"That's what I did say. He asked you."

"Brenda, you're not overtired or overwrought or—"

"I'm not over anything. He asked you."

"He invited me to his house?"

"Yes. If you want the truth, it was my suggestion. He turned it down and then went away and thought about it and came back and said you were to come. You're to have your mother's room."

"If he changed his mind once, he could change it again."

"Are you coming or aren't you?"

"If you're sure he won't throw me out the moment he sees me—"

"Will you say Yes, or, alternatively, No?"

"Of course I'll come. Only—"

"Only what? Money, I suppose?"

"Yes. Total lack of."

"Have you got the train fare?"

"Single, yes. I haven't had any pay since the middle of April, and I won't get any until the cash box comes back."

"Take a single ticket and I'll pay for your taxi up from the station."

"You're wonderful. Shall I come on the morning or the afternoon train?"

"Morning. Is tomorrow too soon?"

"A bit."

"Then make it the day after."

"Can I bring my violin?"

"No, you can't. He'd go out of his mind. And tell your friends not to keep ringing you up. And don't wear anything too Londonish—it was partly that that upset him last time."

"I wear what's being worn. Does he expect me to dress in tweed suits and beetle-crushers?"

"Yes. Have you got enough money to buy me a carton of cream. The Devonshire kind—clotted."

"I might have."

"Then bring it. Good-bye. It'll be nice to see you."

Chapter
Three

THE RAILWAY STATION at Ellstream had been designed on a strictly functional plan. A broad strip of concrete served as a double platform, arrows indicating A to the east and B to the west. Bordering the concrete on one side were the station buildings, all without exception ugly and unheated. Improvements had from time to time been proposed, and voted against, for there had been several attempts on the part of the Government to close this branch line—which was more a loop line, since it left the main line at a junction seventeen miles from Ellstream and joined it again after having performed a slow semi-circle round the market towns of the district. At each threat to deprive the farmers of their railway, the outcry had shaken the walls of Westminster—and had caused the cancellation of all local plans for improvement.

The trains were as stark as the station—old rolling stock with engines that were the delight of small boys all along the route, and whistles that scattered the cows grazing in the fields. Passengers were for the most part farmers and their wives. There were two first- and two second-class carriages; the rest of the train consisted of goods wagons laden with vegetables or livestock.

It was a cold, wet morning when Paul drove down to meet his grandmother's guest. It was also the weekly market day, and the concrete strip, usually almost deserted, was crowded with women weighed down with shopping baskets full of produce bought from the market stalls in the town square. Nobody was disposed to give way and let Paul through, for besides being market day, this was neighbours' meeting day, and the chattering groups were not easy to separate.

The station bell that notified the town of the train's approach had rung; the train whistle could be heard in the distance. The station master, pushing his way through the crowd, found himself next to Paul and nodded.

"Mornin', Mr. Merrion. Nasty wet day. You'll be meeting someone, right?"

"Yes."

"Staying long this time, sir?"

"About a couple of weeks," Paul said, and knew that the friendliness he met everywhere in Ellstream was due to his being regarded as one of the town's sons; hadn't his grandfather been one of its most generous benefactors, and hadn't his mother been born and reared here, and married from St. Ewold's by the same vicar who had christened her? Thus Paul knew that he was, so to speak, in. People like Mr. Ainstey, he was aware, would never be in.

Waiting for the train to draw into the station, he had a fairly clear idea of the type of girl he had come to meet; his grandmother's candidates could be relied on to run to form. He could take for granted race and creed and a not-too-brilliant level of intelligence, and no concessions to permissiveness. If anybody refused to believe that there were still girls today who paled at the first friendly pat, his grandmother knew where they were to be found.

The train, coming alongside, halted with a tired sigh. The doors of the passenger accommodation swung open, and there was a rush to disembark. When most of the newly arrived had stepped on to the platform, he saw a girl appear in the doorway of the first-class carriage almost in front of him, and instantly labelled her Miss Purvis. She was tall, and built on generous lines. She had brown eyes, and dark hair arranged neatly around a clear-skinned, square-jawed face. She could not be called pretty, but in a rather heavy way, she was handsome. Her bearing was one of complete self-assurance.

He could not go nearer; the passengers waiting to board the train had surged forward and were pressing impatiently towards the doors. Miss Purvis, still standing at one of them, continued to look over the heads of the crowd, ignoring requests to move out of the way. As she appeared deaf, stronger measures were resorted to; just as she caught sight of Paul, she was swept back into the carriage and lost to view.

He did not feel sympathetic; she shouldn't have held up the traffic. He felt himself being carried forward by the throng, fought the current, stopped at the door of her carriage and saw her reappear, her hair disordered but her self-assurance unimpaired. Firm hands reached up to pull her out; two suitcases, a mackintosh and a sheaf of newspapers were thrust out after her.

He did not think it a time for polite greetings. He seized the suitcases before they could be knocked over and trampled on, and indicated by a jerk of his head that she was to follow him. When she caught him up at the edge of the crowd, he spoke.

"Sorry about that," he said. "Market day."

"So I gathered when I got out of the other train at the junction." Her voice was rather loud, her enunciation very clear, her tone indulgent with a touch of patronage: the voice of his long-forgotten cub-mistress. "If your grandmother had only told me the entire countryside would be travelling, naturally I would have changed the day. How did you manage to identify me? I knew you at once, of course; I've seen your picture in the paper lots of times. But my picture's never in anything but the local rags when I'm riding in one of those country affairs, so I didn't think you'd be able to spot me. Do you ever go to the junction to meet people?"

"No."

"Well, I know petrol's precious and all that kind of thing, but this last part of the journey's a bit much, if you follow me. Your grandmother said her car was going to fetch my uncle, and you'd be coming to meet me, but I wish she'd asked you to go to the junction. How is she, by the way?"

"She's very well, I think."

He was steering her towards his car, but when they reached the end of the roof that protected the station, the heavy rain brought him to a halt. He put down the suitcases with relief; she had probably had to pack enough for her visit to his grandmother and for her trip with her uncle, but his arms felt as though he had been carrying crates of lead. Perhaps the cases were full of riding boots. The larger one could have fitted a saddle.

"Wait here, will you? I'll bring the car nearer," he said.

"Oh, heavens above, I'm not afraid of a little rain!" She gave a hearty laugh that set his teeth on edge. "I'll put on my mac and come with you and—"

"No. There's no point in getting soaked."

He turned up the collar of his mackintosh and walked away, ignoring her protest that he was making an unnecessary fuss. The hearty type, he diagnosed morosely; one of those girls it was difficult to like, but almost impossible to dislike. She radiated goodwill; all she lacked was the ability to gauge audience reaction.

He passed the taxi stand; it was empty. On a bench beside it waited a girl, and as he went by, her eyes followed him, and there was surprise in them. Paul Merrion. What was he doing here? Well, of course his mother lived here, and so did his grandmother—but where was his fiancée? That girl standing over there waiting for him was no Diana Framley. He didn't look at all like a man who had just become engaged—yet the Greek girl who worked at the hairdressing salon to which Diana Framley went had said that the engagement was definite; Miss Framley had told them so, and had shown all the girls her engagement ring.

So who was this girl? Sister? No, his sister was married and lived in America. Cousin? If so, he ought to give her a few hints on how to dress. She couldn't be short of money —look at those expensive suitcases—so why that outfit, which should have been hanging in a Fashions of Yesterday display? Age? Hard to tell, anything between eighteen and twenty-eight, but you could read her past like a book: prefect, head of form, head of house, head of school, captain of lacrosse, winner of the shield for the best all-around athlete, patrol leader, good with the little ones . . .

Her interest faded. From a bulging flight bag on the bench beside her she extracted a paperback, but she did not open it. Indolent by nature, she derived a good deal of pleasure from watching others, who seemed to her to expend far too much energy in organizing matters that could be left to arrange themselves. She had a theory, not clearly defined, that things happened whether you exhausted yourself making them happen, or sat back and waited for them to happen. People gave you a lot of advice about bestirring yourself and using your elbows to get what you wanted out of life; it sounded all right, but a lot of it turned out to be wasted effort.

Her musing was interrupted by the voice of the station master, calling to her from the edge of the concrete strip.

"No use waiting for a taxi, Miss," he informed her. "You won't get no taxis now. They take the passengers off this train, and then they has to go and have their dinner. If you'll come along to my office, you can give one of the garages in town a ring, and they'll send you out a car. Going far?"

"No. Just up the hill," she called back. "To Mr. Ainstey's."

"Oh, then that's all right. We can soon fix you up." He raised his voice to a shout. "Oh, Mr. Merrion, sir! Young lady here, going up the hill next door to your place. She won't get no taxi till the evening train. Could you take her up the hill?"

Paul turned. He noted without interest that the girl was slim, had fair, softly waving hair, a pair of unusually large, grey, black-lashed eyes and an unruffled air. She spoke calmly.

"No. Thank you, but I can go up on my own. I'll ring up one of those garages. This"—she indicated the flight bag—"is all the luggage I've got, so I can walk up when it stops raining."

His answer was to walk back to the bench and pick up the flight bag.

"Come on," he ordered.

"Deaf?" she enquired mildly. "I told you—I can walk."

He glanced up at the rain-laden sky.

"Wait here," he directed. "It'll be a tight fit, but we're not going far."

He backed the car to the place at which Yolanda Purvis

was waiting. Then he got out and waited for the two girls to join him.

"Oh, three of us?" Yolanda said. "Hello. My name's Yolanda Purvis, and as I see you don't know him, let me introduce Paul Merrion. You're—?"

"Lydia Cresset. I'm Mr. Ainstey's stepdaughter," she added to Paul.

He leaned into the car to put the flight bag into the luggage compartment.

"Don't maltreat that," Lydia asked him. "It's got—"

"A bomb?" He threw the bag onto the suitcases. "Let's get going."

Lydia, being nearest, got in first. Perhaps it was the contrast with the other girl, he thought, that gave her that willowy look. Yolanda followed her, and Paul took his place at the wheel.

"I saw you at the junction," Yolanda told Lydia. "It's a pity we didn't get into the same carriage."

"Couldn't have done," Lydia said. "I was travelling second-class."

She spoke absently; her mind was busy with speculation. That notice in the evening paper two nights ago—could it have been true? Reading it, she had thought that the reporter had got his facts wrong. A girl didn't go off to Venice with her mother the moment she got engaged. But it looked as though she'd done just that; she certainly wasn't here, and he was, in a mood any man would be in in the circumstances. How, she wondered, could any girl, having got a man like this one, leave him lying round? It was very odd, but people up in those dizzy social heights did things that people in the lower brackets—herself, for instance—wouldn't dream of doing. Or would be afraid to do. Or couldn't afford to do. If she ever got a man like Paul Merrion, she'd leave Venice to the gondoliers. And in the meantime he was on one side of her, glooming, and on her other side was this outsize gym mistress, talking nonstop.

"I'm only staying about a week," Yolanda was explaining. "Lady Charlotte thought it would be a good idea if I joined my uncle—he's staying with her, too—so that he and I could start off together on this lecture tour he's going to do. I act as his secretary while he's lecturing—he's terribly absentminded, and if he's on his own, he's apt to forget his notes, or even forget the date of the lecture. I'd like to drive him, but he's petrified in cars. He'd certainly never be able to get himself on a train in time, if I didn't go with him. The rest of the time," she went on, oblivious to the total lack of interest shown by the listeners, "I train horses. One of these days, I'm going to start a riding school, but I'll have to wait until my uncle's given up lecturing." She leaned forward to include Paul in the conversation. "Nice car, this. It's the latest model, isn't it?"

"Yes."

"I thought so. I'm pretty good at spotting that kind of thing. A cousin of mine has the last model, and it has a slightly smaller bar—you can't see it until you press a button, and then it slides out like a little cupboard. I suppose this one does, too." She experimented, found that it did, and then looked out at the rain-washed streets. "Funny little town. Damp, I'd say, built so close to the river. But your grandmother's up on the hill, isn't she?"

"Yes."

"And your mother, too."

"And my stepfather, three," Lydia murmured.

"My uncle," Yolanda proceeded, "told me that there was an old ruin on Lady Charlotte's land, but she had it pulled down. He was sorry about that, because he said that even if it was ugly, it was probably interesting. He thinks all ruins are interesting."

Paul, with an effort, roused himself from his stupor of boredom.

"Not this ruin," he said.

"But it had been there for two hundred years, my uncle told me. He said the owner never lived in it—only his wife, who was some kind of Indian princess. Isn't that right?"

"It was never proved that she was his wife, and the princess status was also doubtful," Paul answered. "She certainly came here before he did, and built the house and the brick tower on one side of it. Her husband never saw them because the coach he was travelling in overturned just outside Ellstream. They still call that curve of the river Turnover Bend."

"I call that *fascinating*," Yolanda said with enthusiasm. "I'm frightfully keen on local history wherever I go. I'm told I have a flair for recreating the past. You won't believe this, but I can build up, actually build up a picture of things as they were long ago. I'm often asked why I don't write plays—historical plays, I mean. The answer is, of course, that I'm far too busy doing other things. Though I do sometimes jot down ideas as they come to me in odd moments."

She paused—for breath, Lydia thought, but Paul sensed an air of expectancy.

"Interesting," he supplied.

"Most," said Lydia.

"What I should have been, of course, is an archivist. That, I feel, would have been my—shall we say—*métier?* Oh, isn't that a nice view of the town? It looks far more attractive from up here, don't you agree? From here, you can't see all those rather uninteresting little streets. What a pity I didn't leave out my camera. I've taken some rather good photographs which I enter now and then for competitions—I got a third in the last 'Scenic England,' and they asked me to submit more. That's my trouble —I'm interested in too many things, and the result—Oh, is this your grandmother's house?"

"Yes. I'm dropping you first," Paul told her, "and then going to Mr. Ainstey's." Thus using Lydia Cresset, he added to himself, as an excuse to get away.

He left Lydia in the car and delivered Yolanda into his grandmother's care. She thanked him and reminded him that she would expect his mother and himself to dinner at eight. He returned to the car and in silence drove away. The removal of Yolanda had left a welcome peace.

"Might have been shyness," he suggested after a time.

Lydia nodded.

"Probably. What's an archivist?"

"Someone who looks after archives, or public records. How long are you staying?"

"Not long. My stepfather can't stand me for long. And it depends on whether my job starts again or not."

"What's your job?"

"Playing the violin in a string quartet. The leader, by name Kellerman, is off on one of his intermittent elopements, and this time, he took the money that should have paid the salaries. His wife's looking for him; in the meantime, I'm out of a job."

"There's not much to do in Ellstream."

"I can take up local history, like what's her name, Yolanda. Your grandmother pulled down that brick tower as well as the ruined house, didn't she?"

"Yes. It was even uglier than the house."

"My stepfather thought the bricks were nice. He found a lot of them lying in a corner of your grandmother's land. They'd been thrown there by the builders when they pulled down the tower."

"The remains of the tower. The top part had crumbled. It was never very high—it didn't really deserve the name of tower. No more than fifteen feet. What did your stepfather do with the bricks?"

"He built a sundial in the middle of his lawn. But I don't think he asked permission before taking the bricks, so perhaps you'd better not mention it to your grandmother."

"If they were hers, and he used them, there'll be no need to mention it. She'll know. She—" He paused. "What's the matter?"

She had turned on the seat and was reaching for the flight bag. For a moment her face was close to his own, and he thought that he had never seen eyes so large and so lovely. She lifted the bag and placed it on the seat between them. Peering into it, she gave a resigned sigh.

"Too late," she said.

"Too late for what?"

"To save my aunt's cream. The clotted kind which she can't buy here. I brought some and I put it into the flight bag when I was waiting on that bench at the taxi stand, but you threw the bag into the back and . . . Look."

He took his eyes off the road and glanced down at the carton of cream she was holding. It had burst, and she was trying to push the bulging sides together. The car went round a curve of the hill, and a large patch of cream spurted on to the knee of his trousers.

"Hell," he said furiously, and drew the car to the side of the road. He switched off the engine and reached for his handkerchief.

"I tried to tell you about it," she reminded him, "but you said it was a bomb, and threw it at the back. I don't think it's any use dabbing at it. We're almost at my stepfather's house; you can come in and clean yourself up."

"I'll go home and clean myself up, thank you."

Starting the car, he felt resentfully that for a girl who had ruined an expensive pair of trousers, she had shown an attitude of unjustifiable detachment. He hated fuss, but he thought that a little more regret on her part wouldn't have come amiss. He had rather liked her calm, relaxed air, but that was before she had ruined his trousers.

When he stopped the car before Mr. Ainstey's door, it opened and Brenda, purse in hand, appeared. She opened the purse, took a second look at the car and closed it again.

"I was going to pay the taxi," she said. "Glad to save the fare. Nice to see you, Lydia. You're Paul Merrion, aren't you? We've never met, but I've caught glimpses of you on some of your comings and goings. What have you done to the knee of your trousers?"

"He didn't. I did," Lydia said. "There went your clotted cream."

"You might tell your niece," Paul informed Brenda, "that an overfull flight bag isn't the best place for a carton of cream."

"I'll tell her. Lydia, make a note. Come in, Mr. Merrion, and I'll do my best to clean it up. This way."

He hesitated, but she was already leading the way into the house. He followed, and in the kitchen she wiped off as much of the cream as she could, and handed him a towel to dab on the wet patch.

"Thanks," he said. "Now I'll be going."

"Give my compliments to your mother," Brenda said. "We don't often meet, but it's nice to know she's a neighbour."

He was at the door. Lydia spoke.

"Why don't we have a drink before you go?" she suggested. "A sort of celebration."

"What are we going to celebrate?" Brenda asked in surprise. "Your return after so long?"

"No. Mr. Merrion's engagement. He got engaged the other day."

There was a slight pause. There was no change in Paul's expression, but something told Lydia that she had been indiscreet. She was sure of it when he spoke—his voice was cold.

"It hasn't been announced," he said. "How did you know?"

"Somebody told me. I would have said something about it in the car, but your fiancée wasn't with you, so—"

"My fiancée is in Venice. Who was it who told you?"

"I live in the same house as a Greek girl who works as an assistant at the hairdresser's that your fiancée goes to. She and I share a kitchen, and she talks and I listen. So I get to know about the customers. I'm sorry I mentioned it. I won't broadcast it—but is there any harm in drinking to it?"

"None whatsoever." Brenda spoke firmly. "Come along to the drawing room, Mr. Merrion." She went out of the room, and once more he felt that there was nothing to be done but follow. "It won't be champagne, and it won't be much of anything else, because this is my brother-in-law's drink and he keeps it carefully measured." She crossed the drawing room and opened a cabinet in the corner. "There's gin and there's sherry. Which?"

"Sherry, please," Paul answered.

"And me," Lydia said. "And you, Brenda?"

"As it's a celebration, yes. Make it just an inch; I'm in the middle of cooking lunch."

Lydia raised her glass.

"To you and Miss Framley," she said. "Have fun."

"Thank you." He put a polite question. "Have you met her?"

"No. She and I don't move in the same circles—but I see her in magazines and, as I told you, I get a lot of backstage news."

She longed to ask him why Diana Framley had gone to Venice without him—but she felt that this would be worse than mentioning his engagement. Brenda said good-bye and went back to the kitchen. Lydia went with Paul to the front door and thanked him for bringing her up from the station.

"If I ever get my job back," she said, "you can send me the bill for the trouser cleaning. But if I don't, don't, because . . . look." She pulled out the linings of her trouser suit pockets. "See? Empty. Good-bye."

"Good-bye."

He was gone. She closed the door and walked slowly back to the drawing room to put away the bottle of sherry and remove the glasses. He had gone without any of the usual I-daresay-we'll-run-into-one-another-again-soon speeches. He had gone, saying good-bye as though he meant it, and that would teach her not to mention engagements until they were announced.

As she crossed the hall with the empty glasses, her stepfather entered the house.

"Ah." It was a grunt which he did his best to make a sound of welcome. "Hope you had a good journey?"

"Yes. Thank you."

She had never been able to decide how she should address him. Her sisters called him stepfather, but she thought this awkward. But the cool relations existing between them ruled out anything more friendly.

"You must have come up in one of the garage cars," he said. "That wasn't a taxi I heard driving away."

"No. I got a lift from Mr. Merrion."

He stared at her blankly for a few moments.

"From—?"

"From Paul Merrion."

The words threw his mind into confusion.

"A lift?" He said slowly. "You mean . . . a lift?"

"Yes. He happened to be at the station, so he drove me up the hill."

He stood speechless, marvelling at this miracle of coincidence. She had arrived. He had been at the station. He had brought her up to the house . . .

"I suppose you asked him for a lift because it was raining?"

"No. He offered."

He had offered. She had arrived, he had seen her, he had not been asked for a lift. He had offered her one. This sensational sequel to his scheme made him feel a little giddy, but making an effort to clear his head, he decided that he must do something to move matters one stage further.

"A good-looking fellow," he began awkwardly.

"Yes. Very."

"And of course, not poor. Merrion of Merrion's Bank."

"Yes. Rolling, I daresay."

"And a decent chap, I'd say. There aren't many young fellows of his kind who'd give their mothers so much of their time."

She took a step towards the kitchen.

"Maybe not," she agreed.

"I see you offered him a drink. Quite right, quite right. The least you could do, after he'd brought you all the way up here."

She had reached the kitchen door. Opening it, she spoke over her shoulder.

"Oh, it wasn't for the lift," she explained. "It was a sort of celebration."

Too late, she regretted the words. Hadn't she promised not to broadcast it? Having mentioned a celebration, she would have to state what they had celebrated.

"Celebration—what for?" Mr. Ainstey demanded.

"We drank to his engagement."

"His . . . ?"

"He got engaged a few days ago, but he'd rather it wasn't mentioned. We drank to it."

The door closed behind her. Mr. Ainstey was left alone.

Chapter
Four

IT WAS IMPOSSIBLE for Lydia to understand why Mr. Ainstey, so comparatively cordial on her arrival, reverted without warning to his normal unfriendliness of manner. So sour had he become by lunchtime that she went into the dining room and removed the plates she had laid opposite to his at the table.

"I'm going to eat with you, as I was going to do before you talked me out of it," she told Brenda, joining her in the kitchen. "What did I do to him?"

"Nothing. He's brooding. He'd die rather than admit he misses your mother—but he does."

Mr. Ainstey was not brooding. He was out in the garden reviewing his abortive plan and realizing with horror how near he had come to making a fool of himself. Never again, he promised himself, would he hatch any schemes. Once was enough. The thing had collapsed, and he was left saddled with the stepdaughter he most detested, and as no definite limit had been fixed for her visit, she would probably be here until she decided to go away and attach herself to a new quartet.

His eyes went to the sundial, and his expression cleared. There was something he could claim to have done successfully. That fellow in the cottage, Mrs. Merrion's brother-in-law, had called it charming, and so it was. He'd get on with making the base; he'd leave the garden alone for a few days and fetch some more of those bricks and make a narrow circular kind of terrace at the base of the sundial. He looked at his watch: twelve-ten. Lunch in fifty minutes. As he allowed no change in the weekly menus, it would be lamb chops, baked potatoes, peas, stewed fruit and custard. Hard to understand people who were always lunching or dining in restaurants; why couldn't they stay at home, as he did, and eat simple, healthy, home-cooked meals, with fresh produce straight out of the garden? He would have his lunch and then he would spend an hour or so in his study and then, round about four o'clock, when Lady Charlotte's head gardener and his assistants were out of the way having their tea, he'd go up and get those bricks. It was a pity he wouldn't have a clear field, as he had had on the last occasion on which he'd helped himself to some. The old lady had been away and the gardeners had been taking advantage of her absence to do as little as possible. But it was not likely that anybody would be up in that remote corner of the grounds.

He was relieved, on entering the dining room, to see that only one place was laid. He enjoyed his meal and felt better after it. Sipping coffee, he got out pen and paper and made a few rough sketches for the base of the sundial.

Shortly after four o'clock, he was painfully pushing a brick-laden wheelbarrow over the scrub, boulders and miniature waterfalls that formed a natural barrier between his land and Lady Charlotte's. His conscience had asked one or two awkward questions, but he had had little difficulty in justifying his action. Robbing? Most certainly not. A man like himself, a man of integrity, a man who throughout his office career had been too scrupulous even to make use of the firm's writing paper for his own letters—robbing? A man who never failed to keep his proper place in a queue, a man who had always scorned to invent pretexts for leaving the office during working hours—robbing? Absurd. The bricks had been up here for years, unused, unwanted, the debris from the demolished brick tower—why should he not make use of them?

Mr. Ainstey had come upon the bricks when he had been walking among the stone and scrub at the highest point of his land. There was no more than a low wall marking the boundary, and over this he had peered covetously at the very things he needed for his projected sundial. He knew nothing about bricks in general, but he had realized that these were not the common run used by contemporary builders; they were a deep rose colour, and seemed to darken in sunlight. As soon as he heard that Lady Charlotte had left on a visit to London, he helped himself to the number he needed.

This afternoon, he had hesitated before beginning the task of fetching the bricks. Perhaps it would be wiser to wait until it was dusk? He decided that the terrain was difficult enough without adding bad visibility to his problems. If anybody caught him—he rejected the word —if anybody *saw* him, it would be better to be seen in open daylight than at dusk. He had ample time; the gardeners took at least three quarters of an hour over their tea, and they would hardly be working so far away from the flower gardens.

He had got out the wheelbarrow from the shed and wheeled it as noisily as possible past the kitchen, to give his sister-in-law and stepdaughter the idea that he was on his way to the kitchen garden. He then made a detour and began the difficult rise at the back of the house. He had calculated that he needed to make three journeys.

The first two were made not without hard pushing and pulling, but without incident. On his return from the third foray, however, he had got the wheelbarrow over the low dividing wall and was about to begin the descent when he heard a voice.

"Oi!"

He did not pause; a glance over his shoulder told him that this was not the head gardener, but the younger of his two assistants—a boy of fifteen or so, a Billy Bunter of a boy bursting out of his clothes. He was walking slowly along on the other side of the wall, following Mr. Ainstey's progress with a glare of suspicion.

"Oi!" he called again. "Come back with them bricks."

Mr. Ainstey increased his pace and threw a reassuring sentence over his shoulder.

"That's all right, m'boy." He was glad to hear that his voice, although breathless, had a confident ring. "Quite all right."

The infernal fellow, he saw, was still moving.

"Them's not your bricks," he shouted.

Mr. Ainstey opened his mouth to say that he was certain Lady Charlotte would not mind. What he said, to his annoyance and humiliation was:

"It's all right. I've got permission from her ladyship."

"Nobody told me nothing about—" began the boy, but his eyes being fixed on Mr. Ainstey, he failed to see the boulder in his path, and fell over it. By the time he got to his feet, Mr. Ainstey was far enough away to be able to disregard further challenges. He pushed his way angrily down the hill, his clothes showing signs of their struggle with thorns and branches; exhausted and apprehensive, he added this load to the two behind the woodshed, and removed the dust from his jacket and trousers. Walking to the house, he tried to assess the result of his encounter with a member, however humble, of Lady Charlotte's staff. An aggressive lad. The kind that enjoyed making trouble. The only consolation was that he would take his complaint—if he took it anywhere—to the head gardener, and it was not likely that the loss of a few bricks would be reported to his mistress.

His eyes fell on the pegs which he had placed round the sundial to mark the extent of the base; his weariness and his uneasy conjectures were forgotten. He worked for an hour, and then decided to go down and see if he could get a game of bridge at his club.

Lydia, in the kitchen helping Brenda with the preparations for dinner, watched him go.

"I passed him in the hall ten minutes ago," she said, "and he pretended I wasn't there. We shouldn't have given Paul Merrion that drink—that's what did it."

"Perhaps. I'm sorry," Brenda said. "I mean, I'm sorry about bringing you here. I thought that as he'd sanctioned it, he'd make some effort to be civil."

"He's been up the hill getting bricks. Did he ask permission this time?"

"Not as far as I know. What the owner's eye doesn't see, permission isn't asked for."

"Do you think he invited me here to tell me he's going to stop my allowance?"

"No, I don't. If that was his reason, he'd have got it off his chest by now."

Lydia gave up the pretense of helping, and settled herself on a stool.

"Sometimes," she said broodingly, "I feel I'd almost rather get married than go on taking money from him."

"What's stopping you?" Brenda enquired. "According to your mother, it isn't lack of opportunity."

"I've never met anybody who made me feel I'd like to spend my whole life with them, that's all. Like you."

"I wasn't the marrying type."

"Is there a marrying type?"

"Well, there's a type of woman who's better off married. Women who want children, for instance. Women who want a home—like your mother. Women who have to fall back on men because they've no other way of achieving security. If a woman doesn't want children, is happy in a little flat of her own and can earn a decent living, what does she want with a man?"

"Some fun?"

"If she wants that kind of fun, she doesn't have to go far to find it. That's one industry in which you'll never find men going on strike. As far as you're concerned, you're not, in my opinion, equipped to make a decent life for yourself. Look at you: twenty-two, scraping away at a violin in a fourth-rate quartet, living in a dingy little room . . . Isn't there any man you know who looks as though he'd make you a good husband?"

"Nobody like Paul Merrion." She leaned forward, elbows on the counter, chin on her hands, and spoke dreamily. "I wouldn't mind a man like that in my life. How can that girl go away and leave him?"

"If they're engaged, she made sure of him before leaving."

"There's something that doesn't fit. He doesn't look like a man who's just got engaged. Did you think he did?"

"He didn't look too enchanted when you mentioned his engagement, but that doesn't prove anything. Let him sort out his own problems. We're discussing yours. Who are these men you run around with?"

"Well—just men."

"Who, for instance?"

"There's the cello player in the quartet. He thinks it would be sensible if we got married."

"What's he like?"

"Not bad. A bit pessimistic. He keeps saying the country's on its last legs."

"Is he doing anything to prop it up?"

"He goes to a lot of political meetings. He takes me along sometimes."

"Which party?"

"It's a new one that some of his friends have formed. It's called the Forward Movement and they're trying to do away with money and—"

"Leave him for the moment. Who else?"

"There's a doctor who's just gone into partnership with my doctor. He's a widower with three children and—"

"Next?"

"There's a travelling salesman who—"

"Next?"

"There's a man who's taking his law exams. He wants to marry me and live in Wales."

"Has he got any money?"

"No. He's kept by a rich aunt."

"Young and healthy?"

"Him or the aunt?"

"The aunt."

"Yes."

"Next?"

"What does it matter? I'm perfectly happy as I am."

"That's your trouble. That's always been your trouble. Contentment's the enemy of progress, and you've been cursed with a contented disposition."

"Why don't you study my life from another angle? The quartet isn't fourth-rate; it's almost first-rate. The room I live in isn't dingy; it's got a window looking out on to what I call a garden—it's really a square of concrete, but I've put tubs of flowers out there, and they look nice. I've got a comfortable bed. I've got a bicycle and I can get out into the country when I can find time. I like my job and I like the people I meet and I like living in London, even the Pimlico part of it. So I'm happy, so you can relax. Who's the man in Mrs. Merrion's guest cottage?"

"Her brother-in-law. I've never met him—in fact, I've never seen him. He was here about three years ago. He's a bad hat."

"A what?"

"The family black sheep. He runs up bills in the town and leaves them to be paid by Mrs. Merrion. He's not here often enough for stories about him to get round, but the tradespeople know him."

"Why doesn't Lady Charlotte pay the bills? She's his mother, isn't she?"

"They're not on speaking terms. Look, instead of sitting there doing nothing, could you roll out this pastry?"

"Apple pie? Nice. How thick do I have to roll?"

"Fairly thin. I wish I didn't worry about you."

"Still? I've just told you what a happy life I lead."

"That's all very well." Brenda's tone was halfway between disgust and despair. "You don't seem to have any thought for the future. You've been going along for years, ever since you left that music college, contented as they come, but getting nowhere. You don't seem to make any effort to *do* anything. Bone lazy, you are. Even admitting that your sisters got most of the brains, you were supplied with a good fund of sense, so why don't you use it? How much longer are you going to cruise round on your bicycle leading the kind of life that anybody could have led without the benefit of your education and advantages? Don't you want to make something of yourself?"

74

"Tell me what. I couldn't be a better violinist, that's certain; I've reached what my violin teacher called the limit of my capacity. Do you really want me to get married for the sake of that security you were talking about?"

"You ought to look at the future—the distant future. Your stepfather'll die one day, and he'll leave what he's got, which isn't much, to your mother. She'll get this house, so she and I will be able to end our days with a roof over our heads. What your mother will leave when she dies will be this house and not much else—to be divided between you four girls, with a proviso that you don't turn me out of it. So where and what are you? You're a middle-aged woman trying to get a job playing the violin. No home, no money; just a bicycle."

"Are you trying to scare me?"

"Yes."

"Into marriage?"

"What else is there? Living the way you do, on your own, with nobody to question what you do, nobody to keep an eye on you, nobody to— "

"Oh Brenda, help! The pastry's fallen into the pie."

Brenda, with difficulty, got it out again.

"You're no help," she said in disgust. "Go away while I finish getting the dinner ready."

"Shall I bring you a nice drink of his sherry?"

"No. Just go away."

Lydia went into the garden. Gazing at the sundial, she did her best to picture the dark future predicted for her by Brenda, but saw nothing to alarm her. The trouble with women of Brenda's age, she mused, was that things were only beginning to loosen up when they were young. They thought they were broad-minded, but all they knew about today's kind of living was the fringe.

Men. There were always men around, but she had to admit that there were no Paul Merrions among them. It

75

wasn't his money that made the difference; it was a number of other things. Perhaps she was not drifting, but waiting—waiting for a Paul Merrion to go by, stop and pick her up. Someone who—

"Good evening."

The voice came from the other side of the flowering shrubs between the garden and the guest cottage. Standing close to the border was a man. He raised a hand, and then spoke.

"Couldn't neighbours get better acquainted?" he asked.

She went closer.

"You're Paul Merrion's uncle?"

"I am. Who are you?"

"Mr. Ainstey's stepdaughter. My name's Lydia Cresset."

"If I get another chair, will you come across the dividing line and have a drink? It's a lovely evening and you seem, like me, to have time on your hands. I had planned to go up to my sister-in-law's house and invite myself to dinner, but there's nobody at home."

When she reached the cottage garden, he had brought out a cushioned chair, a small table and a selection of bottles.

"Did Paul tell you I was staying at the cottage?" he asked.

"No. My aunt did. She warned me, but she wasn't clear what about." She settled herself in the chair. "You tell me."

He paused in the act of opening a bottle of olives, and considered.

"Well, I borrow money, and as a rule don't return it. That's my . . . I was going to say my cardinal fault, but perhaps I'm getting mixed up. There are cardinal virtues, aren't there? Justice, prudence, temperance, fortitude.

I'm just, I'm prudent, I'm temperate and I can claim to possess a certain degree of fortitude. But people disapprove of me because I live on the fruits of other people's labour."

"I've got friends who do that. They seem to me to work harder at it than they'd have to work at a regular job. If you want to borrow money from me, you can't, because I haven't any. How long are you going to stay in the cottage?"

"I've no idea. I go by the weather—the signs. Slight breezes—those are hints which I can ignore. The hints become more pointed; if a storm seems to be blowing up, I pack my briefcase, and depart."

"Your suitcase, you mean."

"No. No suitcase. A briefcase. Travelling with a briefcase, you inspire confidence. Inside it are not important papers, of course; just my changes of shirt and pyjamas. But nobody knows that. Seeing me, slim, grey-haired, handsome, of obviously good background, they take me to be an executive—in trains, entering pubs, accosting my friends or addressing strangers. That's what I call preparing the ground."

"It's an idea. I'll pass it on to my friends."

He asked what she would like to drink. As she seemed uncertain, he recommended rum and orange.

"It's my favourite evening drink," he said. "Fresh orange, of course. Half a teaspoonful of brown sugar; then almost fill the glass with soda—so. And then add the rum." He brought her the glass. "Try that."

She sipped, and nodded approvingly.

"Lovely. Thank you."

"I'll make myself one too. Did your stepfather complain to you about the noise my friends made the other night?"

"No. We're not really friendly. Like you and—"

She stopped abruptly; smiling, he finished the sentence.

"Like my mother and myself?"

"Sometimes I talk too much. I'm sorry about you and her. Not getting on well with your stepfather seems natural in a way, but mothers and sons . . . that's different."

"Have you met my mother?"

"No."

He looked surprised.

"She's been a neighbour for some time," he pointed out.

"I don't come here often. This is my first visit for two years. And my stepfather doesn't believe in getting friendly with the neighbours. He thinks all social exchanges ought to be confined to clubs."

"In these servantless days, not a bad idea. How are you going to amuse yourself while you're here?"

"If you were in my place, how would you amuse yourself?"

"If I were your age and sex, I'd look round for a young man to keep me company. I've got a good-looking nephew I can offer you."

"How can you offer him? He's engaged," she said, and saw him come upright in his chair.

"Engaged?" he repeated in astonishment. "Paul—engaged?"

"You didn't know?"

"No."

"He didn't say anything?"

"No."

"Then that makes twice in two minutes that I've talked too much. I told him I wouldn't broadcast it, but I thought the members of his family would know."

"Do you know who the girl is?"

"Only by name. She's called Diana Framley."

"Diana Framley? Are you sure you've got it right?"

"Of course I'm sure. It wasn't in the papers, but I live with her hairdresser's assistant, and that's how I got the news. I'm sorry I mentioned it."

"Diana Framley!" He leaned back in his chair and looked up at the sky. "He's swimming in deep waters. Brave fellow."

"You know her?"

"I know her mother. I haven't seen Diana since she was about fifteen, but . . . Well, if she's to become a member of my family, perhaps I'd better confine myself to saying that she was already a great beauty."

"And still is, if newspaper pictures are anything to go by. And you don't have to be discreet, because she hits a lot of headlines, and most people, if they can read, can keep up with what she's doing. I'd like to know what his grandmother thinks about it."

"I can tell you. She'll be dead against. She's got what they used to call high moral standards, and she won't believe you if you tell her that moral standards have changed. Drink up and let me give you another."

"No. Thank you, but it's time I went."

"Already? You've only just come."

She put down her empty glass, and rose.

"It can't be time for your dinner," he protested. "Your stepfather isn't back. I saw him go out. I see a good deal through those shrubs. I watched him fetching bricks and starting on whatever it is he's doing at the base of the sundial. Why does he have to cart bricks? Couldn't he have them delivered nearer to the place in which he needs them?"

"He's not buying them. He's borrowing them."

"From—?"

"From your mother. They're the bricks from that tower she pulled down."

"He's using some?"

"Yes."

"Without her permission?"

"Yes. My aunt says that what the owner doesn't see, doesn't hurt."

"I assure you that if he's using my mother's property, she knows—or she won't be long in finding out."

"That's what Paul said. Before I go, could I see the inside of the cottage?"

"By all means."

He led her inside. It was planned on simple lines—a comfortable living room, and behind it three doors leading to bedroom, bathroom and kitchen. Beyond the kitchen was a small storeroom.

"All food and drink supplied by my kind sister-in-law," he said. "She told me she'd put in enough for a week. That's one of those slight breezes I mentioned earlier— the first hint." He watched her regretfully as she walked away. "Must you really go?"

"Yes. Thank you for the drink. Good night."

"If you're free tomorrow morning, why don't you walk down to the town with me? I'm rather an aged companion for you, but I offer myself as escort, and I promise not to borrow money from you."

"I'd like to. Thank you."

"Then it's a date. What time?"

"Eleven?"

"Yes. We'll meet at the gate of your stepfather's house; I don't think he'd be pleased to see me strolling through the barrier and into his garden."

Brenda, preparing to serve dinner, had a brief comment.

"That was quite a session. What's he like?"

"Nice. I'm going to walk down to the town with him

tomorrow morning. He didn't know Paul was engaged
—doesn't that prove there's something wrong?"

"Maybe. But it's not my business and it's not yours
either. Get that dish out of the oven, will you?"

Lydia got it out.

"Don't you and Mother ever get tired of cooking him
two meals a day?" she asked.

"It was one of the stipulations he made when he first
took the rooms in London. If what you mean is that two
healthy women shouldn't use all their time looking after
one healthy man, then you're stepping on to territory I
haven't explored yet. Women seem to be getting steamed
up about the poor imprisoned housewife, chained to the
kitchen sink, but so far, I haven't heard any sensible
suggestions about how to change her lot. That's if she
wants it changed. You hear too much of the moaning and
complaining, and not enough from the women who like
running a home and bringing up children. Somebody's
got to do it, haven't they? Unless they're going to bring in
communal living—no units, just combines. I'll be dead
and gone by then, thank God. No, not those plates—the
warm ones. I wish someone would stand up and say out
loud that running a house is a more rewarding job than
sitting in an office clanking on a typewriter—but there's
company in an office, and not much responsibility, so
when a girl finds herself on her own, cooking and washing
up with no merry colleagues, she gets claustrophobia, and
runs out on the first real responsibility she's ever faced.
You could sweep away most girls in most offices and
replace them in a week. But a wife and mother? Have you
got any sensible suggestions to contribute?"

"Not really. I've never been in an office and I've never
run a house."

"When you do, do it properly. I wish I could get into

81

the homes of some of these reformers. I bet I wouldn't see piles of snowy sheets and pillowcases and towels, and shining silver and gleaming furniture and glistening glasses. Toss that salad, will you? If you're going into town tomorrow, you could do some shopping for me—but what if wicked uncle talks you into giving him the money I give you to buy our food?"

"He promised he wouldn't borrow from me. What's for dinner beside this?"

"Why ask? Just go and study the weekly programme hanging on the back of the door."

"Mixed grill," read Lydia. "Good."

"Better than you think," Brenda said. "I've saved the choice bits for us and given him the rest."

Chapter
Five

LADY CHARLOTTE'S DINNER PARTY was not going well. Paul, looking round the table, could detect no sign of enjoyment on any countenance. On his grandmother's he recognized her customary indifference to the feelings of her guests; she provided comfort, but she did not feel called upon to provide amusements. He had once heard his uncle describe her as a spider, who assembled guests but met them only at meal times.

Tonight's dinner was like all the other dinners he had eaten at her table: perfectly cooked and served, though never deviating from what she called plain English fare. Professor Errol, at all times vague and absentminded, was giving his whole attention to his food. Opposite, eating with almost equal concentration, was Sir William Hallston, a retired barrister who lived in a riverside house two miles from Ellstream. An elderly widower, rotund, bald and bluff, he was a descendant of one of the founders of the boys' school on the hill across the river, and a present

Governor. Next to him sat Yolanda Purvis, whose hearty appetite did not, unfortunately, prevent her from talking. She had given the company her views on pony clubs, beagling, bird watching, karate, yoga, beaver dams, adult education, space travel and gliding; now, peeling an apple, she was giving Mrs. Merrion, who was seated opposite, advice on the rearing of waterfowl. Paul, seated at the foot of the table, did nothing to check the flow; it was clear that the Professor was so accustomed to his niece's monologues that he had ceased to hear them, while Sir William looked grateful for the chance of eating without conversing. He found, as he had found when he met her at the station, that irritation and boredom faded in the light of her invincible cheerfulness and good humour. Abounding in health and vitality, she marched on large, firm feet over the most delicate ground, oblivious to protests, criticism or snubs.

In the drawing room after dinner, Lady Charlotte outlined for the Professor and his niece the interesting things to be seen in town. There was a library with a comfortable reading room. There was a park with a lake, there were two museums. If they wished to walk, there were footpaths over the hills, and on the south side of the river, a towpath which led to the village of Lower Ellstream, four miles away.

"Nothing there that'll appeal to the Professor," Sir William said jovially. "What he'd like would be a few ruins of Eastern temples. None of those round here, Professor. Nothing of the East at all, I'm afraid."

The Professor peered shortsightedly across the room at the speaker.

"There used to be," he said. "What became of the Indian princess?"

"Took sick and died," Sir William answered. "The climate, I daresay. That whole business was mysterious, and it never got cleared up. Was she a princesss? Nobody ever knew. Was she wife or mistress? Nobody knew. All that was known was that she came here, pulled down the Tudor house that was standing on the site, and built a stone house and a brick tower. Ugly, both of them."

"The husband—if he was the husband—was in the East India Company, wasn't he?" the Professor asked.

"Yes. So much is fact. It—"

"And all the rest is guesswork," Lady Charlotte broke in. "When I came here to look at this land, I asked some questions about the history of the ruin that was on it, and got no satisfactory replies. All that the people in the town were interested in was seeing the ruin pulled down."

"Wasn't there any information to be had from the other end—from the people you inherited it from?" Paul asked.

"No. Nothing has ever been definitely known." Her tone indicated her lack of interest in the topic. "The man whose wife or mistress built the house was called Exerton. His heirs were related to somebody in my family, and in time the property came to me. I gave up making enquiries because there were no facts to be discovered—merely rumours and legends and absurd tales of Eastern princesses."

"Now wait a minute." Sir William had known Lady Charlotte for a great many years, and was not in the least cowed by her manner. "Wait a minute. It wasn't rumour or legend about that coach. The husband, the owner of the house, the East India Company fellow, was certainly on his way here. If he wanted to see his princess, he was too late, because she was dead, but it's a fact that the coach overturned and it's also a fact that three people were drowned at that bend of the river, and they were drowned because they were diving for treasure."

"Treasure? What sort of treasure?" Yolanda asked.

85

"Not your uncle's idea of treasure," Sir William said. "No interesting souvenirs from the land of the Moghuls. It was the fact that this fellow Exerton had served all his life in the East that stirred the locals into hoping that he was one of those Nabobs bringing home some of the legendary wealth in his pockets."

"Did anybody find anything?" Yolanda asked.

"If they did, they didn't share it out," Sir William answered. "When they fished out the coach and the bodies of Exerton and the coachmen, there wasn't a diamond or an emerald to be seen. After that, interest died down." He looked across at Paul. "If your grandfather —your mother's father—were alive, he might be able to tell us a bit more. He did a bit of delving. Didn't he, Antonia?"

"Yes, but without much result," Mrs. Merrion said. "The point he thought significant was that the coachman's family came and settled in Ellstream."

"He read a great deal into that," Sir William remembered, "but I never thought there was any special significance in it. The coachman was bringing his master to a house in which they were going to settle; he'd naturally arrange for his family to come and join him."

"But as he died with his master," Mrs. Merrion said, "my father thought it would have been more natural for his family to stay in London, where they belonged. But they came to Ellstream—widow and five children—and settled here. Most significant of all, one of the sons was drowned diving at the place the coach went into the river."

"I never thought that proved anything," Sir William said. "They came here, they heard the rumours about treasure, so naturally one of the sons went diving to see what he could find."

"Perhaps it wasn't the rumours that started them diving," Paul suggested. "How about the theory that the coachman had told his family something that made them suspect the coach was carrying more than the passenger?"

"All guesswork, as I said," Lady Charlotte closed the discussion. "Paul, you must arrange some riding for Yolanda."

"Oh, splendid idea," Yolanda said enthusiastically. "Is there a riding school here?"

"No." It was Sir William who answered. "There used to be, but it closed down. If you want to ride, I've got a couple of horses out at my place. Get Paul to bring you over one morning."

Paul, launching a silent appeal to his mother to get up and leave, said with as much politeness as he could summon that he would drive Yolanda anywhere she wanted to go.

"But if you want to dig up any more historical facts," Sir William told her, "you ought to drop in at the library and have a talk with Miss Clarendon. She knows a lot of local history."

"Good idea," said Yolanda. "Shall we say ten-thirty, Paul? We'll go to the library first, and if there's time after that, perhaps we could drive out and take a look at Sir William's horses."

"Ten-thirty," Paul confirmed.

He telephoned the following morning to ask if she had changed her mind.

"Have you had a look at the weather?" he asked her.

"Oh, you mean the rain? I never let weather worry me. I just put on a mac, and I tie a scarf round my head, and that's that. As a matter of fact, I enjoy being out in the rain. Once when I was—"

"In that case, I'll be round in half an hour."

He put down the receiver and sat staring at it for a few moments. Doing something, he decided bitterly, was better than doing nothing. Driving Yolanda Purvis round was better than letting his mind dwell on the fact that there was still no telephone call from Venice, no telegram, no letter. While he worked out exactly what that meant, he might as well act as chauffeur to anybody who needed one.

Yolanda was ready and waiting, looking businesslike in a mackintosh and head scarf. There was no need for him to get out of the car; Joseph came down the steps with her, screening her under the vast umbrella used to protect guests from sun or rain.

The town did not look its best. Yolanda, in her most decided tone, labelled the inhabitants a drab lot. The rain was coming down with less force; by the time Paul had driven into the car park nearest the library, there was no more than a drizzle.

At the library, they asked for Miss Clarendon. After a brief interval, a tall, angular form appeared from an office enclosed by three ceiling-high bookcases, and came with soft tread to speak to them.

"I am Miss Clarendon." Middle-aged, severe, she spoke in a whisper. "What can I do for you?"

"Good morning. My name's Merrion, and this is—"

"Merrion? Mrs. Merrion's son?"

"Well, naturally, if he's called Merrion," Yolanda said with a hearty laugh, "he'll be the son of a Mrs. Merrion, won't he? I mean to say, he—"

"Hush! Kindly, *kindly* lower your voice," besought Miss Clarendon. "We try to preserve utter peace within these walls. There are students in the reading room. You had both better come to my den. This way, please, as quietly as possible."

They followed her, attempting to walk on their toes. In the den, Miss Clarendon continued to whisper.

"You must be *Paul* Merrion. So silly of me not to have

recognized you. I only saw you once, at a distance—somebody pointed you out to me that last time you were in Ellstream—but I'm not very good at faces. This lady—?"

"Miss Purvis. She's staying with my grandmother, and is interested in local history."

"Oh, really? How nice to meet anyone who wants to delve, as it were, below the surface. I get very upset when people say this is a dull town. It's by no means dull." Miss Clarendon could sound emphatic even when she was whispering. "There are things here of great interest. They spring to mind at once, like that lovely old church, not old by some standards, but old enough to be interesting. They're appealing, you know, for funds, because—"

"Yes, but look here—" began Yolanda.

"Shh!" Miss Clarendon raised a bony forefinger. "We must not make a disturbance. I was telling you about the church. It's believed that some of the old beams came from the trees that were used to build Nelson's ships. As well as that, there's the cross in the square, I don't mean the actual cross, because it isn't there anymore, but you can still see the—"

"What we want—" broke in Yolanda.

"Hush! I beg you to lower your voice. You can still see the steps on which the cross stood, so interesting, fifteenth century, and then there's old Mrs. Cromer's beautiful cottage. Do you know, strangers stop whenever they pass it, it's so charming, with that thatched roof which they say can never be replaced because there aren't any work-men now who know—"

"What about the coach?" Yolanda demanded. She spoke in her normal voice, which was not quiet, and she looked angry. A monologue like Miss Clarendon's, Paul thought, must seem to her an infringement of copyright.

"Coach?" Miss Clarendon repeated in bewilderment.

"We have no coach on view anywhere. It's a pity in a way, because a coach museum gives people, ordinary people, an opportunity to see—"

"The coach that went into the river. *That* coach," said Yolanda.

"Please keep your voice down, Miss . . . Er. I do my best, I do my very best to preserve peace here. We have many booklovers in Ellstream, you know, and I feel I owe it to them to offer a place in which they—"

"And the ruin. And the tower," Yolanda proceeded.

Miss Clarendon subjected her to a long stare to mark her dislike of someone who, after being reproved several times, persisted in shouting.

"If you want information about those," she said frostily, "you must go and see Mr. Morton at the Town Hall. All I have here in that connection is an old print showing the house which used to stand where Lady Charlotte built her house. Will you come this way?"

They followed her out of the den. She led them to a framed print. It was not large, and its details were not clear, but after some moments, Paul was able to trace for Yolanda the contour of the hill, the thick woodland and a clearing on which stood a house of exceptional ugliness. Beside it, low, incongruous, stood the brick tower.

"It was built in 1786," Miss Clarendon told them. "Those two ruins—the house and the tower—did nothing to add to the beauty of this town. What a relief it was to us all to see Lady Charlotte's beautiful house going up!"

She led them back to her den, but Paul, pausing only to thank her, took Yolanda's arm and steered her towards the exit. Going out through the wide glass doors, they found sunshine. As they went down the steps, Paul saw coming towards them his uncle and, to his surprise, Lydia Cresset.

"Good morning. How long have you two known one another?" he enquired.

"We're old and dear friends," Esmond told him. "We met last night." He turned to Yolanda. "I'm Esmond Merrion. You're staying with my mother, aren't you?"

"That's right. Yolanda Purvis. I didn't know you lived here too. Lady Charlotte didn't mention you."

"You shouldn't mention me, either," he advised. "She and I are not old and dear friends. Have you and Paul been looking at books?"

"No. We came to find out a bit of local history, but all we got was someone who shuffled about in felt-soled slippers and told me to hush. Now Paul's going to take me to see Sir William's horses. I don't suppose he—"

She stopped. A very large man, holding two books under his arm, had begun to elbow his way through their group. He was the same height as Paul, but looked twice his width. He had dark, upstanding hair, large horn-rimmed glasses, a mandarin moustache and a bushy beard. His age was about thirty. He spoke in a deep voice.

"Sorry to shove, but you're all standing in the way," he said.

Yolanda had no intention of being pushed. She stood firm, and the man, meeting unexpected resistance, bumped into her with such force that the books he had been holding under his arm fell to the pavement and lay with their pages open in a deep puddle.

"What in hell—" he began furiously, and then stopped. He stood staring at Yolanda, his expression incredulous. When he spoke again, it was in a tone vibrant with loathing.

"Oh, it's you! I might have known. Who but you? I hoped I'd seen the last of you, but here you are again and look!" He pointed to the books. "Ruined. And not mine, either. Library books." He stooped and lifted them and held them out to drip. "You all over, charging round and throwing your weight about and making a ruddy nuisance of yourself and in—"

Paul broke mildly into the furious stream.

"Look, you can't talk to Miss Purvis like that. If you've anything to say—"

"Anything to say? Anything to *say?* First she wrecks an entire Scout camp, and then she knocks two expensive library books into the mud, and you ask me if I've anything to say! Let me—"

"I've got something to say," Yolanda interrupted. "I've never seen this man before in my life. Never."

"Then there's been a mistake, and we can all disperse," Esmond said with relief. He glanced at the knot of sightseers who had gathered. "Give the audience their money back, Paul, and tell them there isn't going to be a performance. If anybody wants me, they'll find me at the Plough."

He walked away. Paul looked at Yolanda.

"Take her away," the stranger entreated. "Remove her."

"I think you'd better remove yourself," Paul suggested. "If you want to go on with the argument, my name's Merrion and I'm staying with my mother up on the hill."

"My name's Roach. Dudley Roach, and I'm up on the hill, too. The other hill. I'm the history master at the school. I'm also in charge of the Scouts."

"Well, Mr. Roach, you're making a mistake," Yolanda told him. "We've never met, so I'd be very glad if you'd apologize for talking to me like—"

"Apologize? Never met? You're Yolanda Purvis, aren't you?"

"Yes, but—"

"Lately the guest of old Lord Rowelling—right?"

"Yes."

"And he owns horses, and you were—"

"I was schooling them."

"So you were. So where did you school them? How much land does Rowelling have round that mansion of his? Four hundred acres? Five? Six? So which particular piece of ground did you choose to school his horses on? If you've forgotten, I'll tell you. You gave orders for fences to be put up on the ground which he'd lent to the troop of Scouts from St. Godric's. Twenty-two tents those boys had put up, in weather conditions pretty much like this morning before the rain stopped. Twenty-two tents, plus a cook's tent plus a latrine tent plus a First Aid tent. That adds up to twenty-five tents, and putting up twenty-five tents is hard work if you're a small boy of ten or eleven. So when all the tents were up, and all the small boys were ready to get round the campfire and get something to eat, what happens? A certain Miss Purvis sends out orders, and fences begin to go up. If I'd been present when the men arrived, I would have broken their fences over their heads—but I had most unfortunately had to drive into the nearest town to check on milk supplies. When I got back, the tents were down and the boys were being marched into a field half a mile away. Making room for the horses. I couldn't get at Miss Purvis to break her neck, because she was—guess where?—out dancing, and wouldn't be back until dawn. And now she wants me to apologize for mentioning the matter."

"I didn't know the first thing," Yolanda declared loudly, "about any Scouts. Nobody told me a word. I was—"

Mr. Roach was glaring down at her.

"Out of my way," he ordered. "And keep out of it in future."

He went with two bounds up the steps. The glass doors

swung slowly shut behind him. Yolanda spoke in bewilderment.

"How can anybody be blamed for something they didn't know about?" she demanded. "Nobody so much as mentioned Scouts. Isn't Sir William one of the school Governors? I think I'll make a complaint about—"

"No, you won't." Paul spoke firmly. "It's over. I'll drive you to his house if you still want to go, but not if you're going to make complaints."

She looked at Lydia.

"Where did Paul's uncle say he was going?" she asked.

"The Plough," Lydia answered. "Wherever that is."

"I'm going there too." Yolanda turned to Paul. "I don't feel like looking at horses. I want to sit down and drink something cool. Which way do I go?"

"First right, second left."

She walked away. Paul was left with Lydia, whose expression throughout had been one of quiet amusement.

"Enjoy it?" he asked coldly.

"Of course. Didn't you? That man Roach ought to have flaming red hair. I wouldn't like to be one of his pupils on the day I'd done a bad history prep. Do you suppose anybody's ever shouted at Yolanda like that before?"

"How would I know? How did you become an old and dear friend of my uncle?"

"I paid him a visit last night, just before dinner. He was sitting in the garden of the cottage, and he saw me wandering about in my stepfather's garden, and invited me over for a drink. Then we made a date to walk down to town this morning. He said he hadn't any money—how is he going to pay for his drink in the pub?"

"He won't. Somebody else will." Rain was falling again, and he put up the collar of his mackintosh. "Want a lift up the hill?"

"Please." She fell into step beside him. "I like him —your uncle, I mean."

"Everybody likes him—in a way, and for a time. What are you stopping for?"

She was looking at the door of the church.

"Do you ever come here?" she asked, walking on.

He looked surprised.

"I accompany my mother if she happens to be going. Why?"

"Then you might know whether I'd be allowed to play the organ while I'm here."

"I thought the violin was your instrument."

"It is, but I play the organ too. I don't often get a chance to play one. Do you know the organist in this town?"

"No. I could find him, if you're serious."

"Of course I'm serious. I've got something now that I don't usually have: time to spare. If this weather's going to continue, what's nicer than sheltering in a church playing the organ?"

"I can think of several things I'd like better." They had reached the car, and he unlocked the doors and opened the one on her side. "You haven't met my mother; how about looking in on her now and staying to lunch?"

"She hasn't invited me."

"She will as soon as I ask her to."

"No. Thanks all the same. How's Yolanda going to get back to your grandmother's?"

"She'll meet my uncle in the pub and ask him to take her. He'll call a taxi and ask to be put down at my mother's gate, and then he'll say he must have left his wallet at the pub and he'll promise to pay her back later. And so on."

"I see. Well, he— Oh!"

"What's the matter? Another burst carton of cream?"

"No. My aunt asked me to do some shopping for her. Mr. Roach drove it out of my head." She was getting out of the car. "Don't wait for me. I'll get back all right. Thanks anyway."

He had got out and was locking the doors again.

"You don't have to come," she told him. "I hate men around when I'm in shops—they lose their temper."

"I am not," he told her, "going to drive up the hill with an empty car. I've lost the passenger I brought down; I'll see that you do your aunt's shopping in record time and then I'll drive you back. Come on."

They were back in less than half an hour. Paul threw the purchases in the back and took the wheel.

"What were you doing in the library?" she asked as they began the journey.

"Local history. It turned out to be more interesting than I'd anticipated."

"Why? I mean, why didn't you anticipate being interested? Your mother was born here and your grandfather was well known here and your grandmother inherited a two-hundred-year-old ruin here. If there was a two-hundred-year-gap in my family history, I'd anticipate being interested in doing some filling in."

"My grandmother said at dinner last night that there were no facts to be discovered about the ruin. I went to the library because somebody thought Miss Clarendon might know something."

"Miss—?"

"Clarendon. The whispering custodian. She didn't produce any facts. All she did was direct me to the Town Hall, where a certain Mr. Morton might know something. All I've gathered so far, from one source or another, is that there was an earlier house on the site—Tudor. Built in 1520."

"Which king was reigning in 1520?"

"Don't you know?"

"I could go back and ask Mr. Roach."

"Every schoolboy—and girl—knows. But they're only interested in how many wives he had, not the date he had them."

"Oh, that one? Henry the Eighth? I could never sort out all the Henrys. Except Henry the Sixth. I remembered him because that was where Joan of Arc came in. I think."

"Interesting reign, that was. A bit like what's going on nowadays. All Henry the Fifth's conquests in France were reconquered by the French and the English were pushed out. We managed to hang on to Calais. To return to local history, I think I'll look in on Mr. Morton tomorrow. He might have some records about the next house that was put up on the site—the one my grandmother pulled down. The one owned by the fellow who was in the East India Company. There's a chance that—"

"Wait a minute. What exactly was the East India Company?"

"Trading corporation authorized by the government to trade in the East Indies. Elizabeth the First granted the company a charter—in 1600, I think. There were other companies—French, Dutch, Danish—but the British got there first and stayed there longest. I think the English company was abolished in the middle of the eighteen hundreds, 1858 or thereabouts. I'll look it up. I've got a book about the Company. I'll lend it to you if you're interested."

"It wouldn't be any good. I'm no good at absorbing facts."

"Not even at school?"

"No. It was a day school in London. I wasn't one of the

prize pupils. People say that the children of older parents are usually bright, or unusually bright, but my three older sisters got all the brains that were going."

"Or made some effort to learn, which you didn't?"

"I worked just as hard as they did at school. But for teachers to make any impression, there has to be something to make an impression on, and in my case there was nothing."

"Where did the violin come in?"

"All the time. They never had to ask me to practise—I practised because I liked it. They thought for a time that I might turn into a musical sensation, but when I was about fourteen, they lost hope. I'm not bad, but I'm not special, and if you're not special in the musical profession, you can't earn much. My stepfather gives me an allowance, but it stops when I marry. What with inflation and so on, he's getting impatient."

"You could tell him to keep the allowance and let you marry in your own good time."

"That's the kind of remark," she said mildly, "that people like you are always making. Have you ever had any money problems?"

"No."

"Have you ever lived in a semi-basement bedroom in a Pimlico boarding house?"

"No."

"You should try it."

"If I did, would I be able to share a kitchen with a Greek girl, like you?"

"You might. And listen to stories about her clients."

Silence succeeded this remark, and she wished that she could recall it. They had been driving slowly, talking about nothing in particular, both conscious of a sense of companionship. So why did she have to drag in that item about the Greek girl's clients? He'd forgotten the Framleys for a time, but now the strained look was back on his face. Why couldn't she learn to keep her mouth shut? She knew what discretion was; why let her tongue run away with her?

"I looked up discretion in the dictionary once," she said after a time. "My aunt said I didn't have enough of it. Looking it up in the dictionary didn't help much, because after saying that it meant prudence, it went on to tell you that you could act according to your own judgment."

"Provided you've got judgment."

"Yes. Provided. Could I go and see Mr. Morton when you go to see him?"

"What do you want to learn from Mr. Morton?"

"The same as you do: dates, facts. My mother lives here; my aunt lives here. My mother wouldn't be interested, because all she thinks about is housekeeping, but my aunt would like to be told something about local history."

"If you want to see Morton, I'll take you, certainly."

"Thank you. But if you take me with you, we have to talk, and we can't talk all the time about local history, because there isn't enough of it, and so every now and then I'll mention the only other subject you and I have in common: your fiancée. It'll slip out the way it did just now. How are you going to feel about that?"

"I might get a little tired of hearing how she has her hair done."

She said nothing. Glancing at her as he went round the last curve of the hill, he saw her heightened colour, but could not tell whether he had hurt her or angered her. He stopped the car outside his mother's gate, switched off the engine and turned to face her.

"I'm sorry about that," he said. "You can say what you like, any time you like. I'd like you to come and see Morton with me. I like your company. You're . . . I don't know the word. Restful? That doesn't sum it up. You fit. So as I said, I'm sorry. I'd like you, if you will, to come in and have a drink—and if you won't stay to lunch, I'll drive you home."

"A drink would be nice. I need one. Thank you."

He drove round to the side of the house, opened the door on her side of the car and waited for her to get out. But she sat motionless, staring across the garden. He saw that she was gazing at the waterfowl enclosure. She spoke on a breathless note.

"Oh! Oh, how . . . how *lovely!*"

"Didn't you know my mother amused herself by breeding ornamental ducks?"

"No." She was out of the car. "Could we go and look?"

They walked to the enclosure and he opened the gate and they walked in and stood at the edge of the water, watching in silence.

"I've never seen anything like these," she said at last, "except in parks and zoos. What's that one over there?"

"Mandarin. The one next to him's an Indian Spotbill."

"You know them all?"

"Most of them. I got tired of telling visitors I didn't know, so I read some of the literature my mother's got on the subject. She keeps buying them because she can't resist the names—the Rosybill diving duck, for example. All the books admit that it's hell to try and classify waterfowl. Some day, if you've time, I'll give you a lecture on subdivisions. I don't know as much about them as my mother does, but I'm catching up."

They went into the house. Mrs. Merrion, doing accounts in the garden room, laid them thankfully aside and turned to greet Lydia, whose manner during and after the introduction, Paul noted, underwent not the slightest change; she had been at ease with him, she was equally at ease with his mother; her first word to her was a quiet, friendly "Hi."

"Just a quick drink," Paul told his mother. "I asked Lydia to have lunch with us, but she's the formal type and has to have a letter from you giving date and time, preferably two or three weeks ahead, as she's pretty booked up, society being what it is in this town."

Mrs. Merrion looked at Lydia with raised eyebrows.

"Very amusing, isn't he?"

Lydia nodded.

"Clever, too. He knows which kings were reigning when."

"How did reigning kings come up?"

"We started off on local history," Paul told her. He brought drinks and carried his to the windowsill. "I took Yolanda to the library—that was local history too, but when we came out, we ran into an outsize history master from St. Godfric's who recognized her as the woman who turned his Scouts out of Lord Rowelling's field because she wanted to school horses. There was a scene. Esmond didn't like it, and departed; Lydia enjoyed every moment. Speaking of local history, I've been thinking about the date on which Exerton's house was built. He must have come back from India just about the time that Warren Hastings was recalled. That fact might have given rise to some of the rumours of treasure, surely?"

"Who was Warren Hastings?" Lydia asked.

"You weren't joking, were you," Paul told her, "when you said you didn't take in much at school. Warren Hastings joined the East India Company and in time became Governor-General of India, but he was recalled in 1785 and impeached. The house that Lottie pulled down was built in 1786. It's not stretching imagination too far to suspect that Exerton might have been on the fringes of some of the fishy business that had been taking place in India, is it? If he was, he wouldn't have come home empty-handed. So perhaps there was something in that coach after all."

"As Lottie said, all guesswork," Mrs. Merrion said. "Lydia, how long are you going to stay in Ellstream?"

"Not long. My stepfather doesn't like guests, above all me. If he doesn't throw me out, I'll have to go back as soon as I get word about my job in London."

"Which is?"

"I play the violin in a string quartet—the Kellerman String Quartet, which I don't suppose you've ever heard of. Mr. Kellerman went off with a girl friend and the funds, and we're waiting for him to come back."

"Couldn't you replace him?"

"There's no need to. It's just a matter of waiting. He goes off about once a year; if the money holds out, his conscience gives in. He couldn't get along without his wife—she's the business head."

"Are your sisters—there are three, aren't there?—all married?"

"Yes. To professors. They're all teaching up in the north. They came to stay here once or twice, but it didn't work, so now my mother goes off every year on a round of visits to us all."

"Leaving your aunt to look after your stepfather?"

"Yes. Which reminds me that I've got her shopping and it's time to give it to her."

"Will you come to lunch one day without that formal invitation?"

"I'd love to. Thank you. And thanks for the drink."

Paul opened the door and was following her out when his mother spoke.

"Paul, where did you leave Yolanda?"

"She went off to join Esmond at the Plough. I expect she'll get him to bring her home."

Yolanda was not with Esmond. She was in a taxi, on her way up to St. Godfric's.

After leaving Paul and Lydia, she had walked to the Plough—but she did not go in. She had been thinking, and as her thought processes were simple and direct, she was not long in making up her mind as to what she was going to do. She walked back to the library and tried to find out how much Mr. Roach would be charged for the damage done to the books he had borrowed. As neither Miss Clarendon nor her assistant were able to tell her, she got into a taxi and directed the driver to the school.

"I can take you up there, Miss; can't wait for you if you want to come down again. I've got to go for my dinner. If you ring up one of the garages, they'll send up a taxi to fetch you down."

"I'll manage," she said confidently.

She had no doubts about the wisdom of her errand. She could do nothing to make up to Mr. Roach for the unfortunate Scout incident, but if he believed her to be responsible for knocking his library books into the mud, she could at least see to it that he didn't have to bear the expense. So she was on her way to pay for the damage, pursuing, as always, a course which she felt to be right and harbouring not the slightest suspicion that others might not see the matter from her point of view. Decision had always been her predominating characteristic, much admired by parents and teachers. A born leader, they called her—inaccurately, since she was not a leader but a pusher.

The rain continued to fall. The taxi driver, on learning that she wanted one of the masters, drove to a detached building behind the school, and stopped. He sounded his horn and an aged porter appeared in the doorway.

"Know where I can find Mr. Roach?" called the driver.

"Who?"

"Roach. R-o-a-c-h."

"Oh, Roach. Not here. Go round to the back and you'll see a hut. He'll be in it."

The hut was visible when they drove round the corner, but only a narrow path led to it.

"You'll have to walk the rest," the driver said. "Better get under cover quick, or you'll be soaked."

She paid the fare, turned up the collar of her mackintosh, got out and ran to the door of the hut and knocked. There was no response. Nor did subsequent thumpings bring anybody to the door.

She moved to a nearby window and looked in. She saw a large, well-equipped gymnasium. At the table in a corner sat Mr. Roach, before him a tall pile of exercise books. She beat a tattoo on the window, and he raised his head, frowning. She pressed her face to the pane and saw his expression change to one of incredulity. He pushed back his chair and crossed the room; she went back to the door, and it opened.

"About time," she said heartily. "Goodness, you must have been concentrating!"

She attempted to step into the room, but his arm barred the way.

"You're not allowed in here," he said. "Who are you looking for?"

"You, of course. Why do you think I—"

"What do you want?"

His tone was brusque, but it did not dent her complacency.

"If you let me in, I'll tell you," she said. "I can't be expected to stand out here dripping, can I?"

He stepped reluctantly aside.

"Make it swift," he directed.

She entered, stamping on the doormat to remove the mud from her shoes. Her mackintosh was dark with moisture; her hair hung in wet strands below the head scarf.

"It's all right; don't worry," she said, although he had expressed no concern. "I've often been a lot wetter than this. I had to come and see you, and the sooner, the better, because after all, you accused me of something I didn't do, and I thought to myself Well, if he's going around saying that about me, it might get back to somebody who knew me, and—"

"Look, I'm working. I came in here to get some peace and to catch up on some backlog. Will you say what you came for, briefly and baldly, and then go away?"

"Well, I could point out," she said reasonably, "that I've gone to a lot of trouble to come up here."

"Too bad. What for?"

"To make some compensation for any loss you—"

"Loss? Compensation? What are you talking about? Will you kindly get to the point, if any?"

"Money is the point. You said I knocked those two library books into the mud this morning. Well, of course I didn't; we merely bumped into one another, so who's to say which of us was responsible for—"

"Yes, yes, yes. Two books in the mud. So what?"

"You said you'd have to pay for them. I didn't want you to have to do that if you thought it was my fault, so I went back to the library and tried to find out how much they'd charge you, but they couldn't tell me, so I had to guess." She paused, plunged a hand into a pocket and brought out a purse. Opening it, she extracted some money and held it out to him. "There you are. I think that's fair. That makes us quits, but if you think—"

"I won't tell you what I think," he broke in, his voice tight with rage. "I should, because it's obvious that nobody has ever told you their opinion of you. But I haven't time. Will you kindly donate that money to some other charity and get the hell out of here?"

He turned on his heel, walked to the table and went back to the work of correcting books. After regarding him with utter perplexity for some moments, she spoke in an aggrieved voice.

"I don't see why you take that attitude, you know. You made it clear this morning that you blamed me, so—"

She stopped. He had risen, and the naked menace on his face penetrated her armour of assurance. He came towards her, and she backed, coming to rest with her shoulders against the vaulting horse.

"Will you get out," he demanded, "or do you want me to throw you out?"

"That temper of yours," she said, "will get you into trouble one day. You went off the handle over the Scouts, and again over the library books, and now you're off again because—"

"Will you—for the last time—go away?"

She gave a resigned shrug.

"Oh, very well. I never met anyone as unreasonable as you before. Will you please show me where the phone is?"

"The what?"

"The phone. I've got to ring up for a taxi. The one that brought me up here couldn't wait because the driver had to go and have his dinner, but he said I could get one to come up and fetch me. Do you know the number of a garage who'd send a car?"

He had difficulty in replying, first because he was having trouble with his breathing, and then because he attempted to say several things at one and the same time. Finally he spoke coherently.

"Do you realize," he asked slowly, "what would happen if someone chanced to lope along and find you here? Do you understand that—No. How could you understand? I'd have to neigh."

He seized her arm, pushed her towards a door, opened it, thrust her inside and closed it after her. She found herself in a cloakroom whose walls were lined with hooks, below which were shelves for boots or shoes.

"Stay in there and don't make a sound," he ordered. "If anyone comes into the gym, stop breathing. I'll be back in five minutes and I'll take you down to the town. There's no time to summon taxis."

She heard the door of the gymnasium bang as he went out. The only light in the cloakroom came from the daylight framing the door. The room smelt of damp clothes.

She heard the outer door open, but she did not move. A moment later, she was released by Mr. Roach. He was wearing a shabby mackintosh.

"This way," he said, and led her to a low window. Opening it, he told her to climb out. "I'm not going to take you the front way. We'd be seen by half the school. If I'm going to be sacked for arranging a session with a girl during teaching hours, it'll be because I arranged one, not because they thought I did. Out you go."

Outside in the rain, leaning against the wall of the gymnasium, she saw an ancient and battered motorbike. Mr. Roach, settling himself on the saddle, jerked his head towards the narrow luggage carrier behind.

"Get on and hang on," he ordered.

For the first time in her life, she found nothing to say. She was having difficulty in believing that she was to be transported on a machine that looked as though it was on the point of falling apart. Going to it and seating herself sideways on the grid, she heard his peremptory command.

"Astride, astride, *astride*. Do you think I can balance a heavyweight like you unless you distribute yourself evenly? That's better. Now hang on."

The only way of hanging on was to place her arms round him. She gripped his waist, dismayed to find its circumference so vast; she could get a firm hold only by clutching his pockets. Her face was pressed sideways on to his mackintosh, which smelt of oil. She was about to tell him that she would prefer to walk, when the machine leapt to life and she forgot everything but the necessity of keeping herself from being thrown off. They were, as far as she could see, taking a wide detour round the school, along narrow, wooded paths that were now open, now enclosed by trees. Potholes became puddles, each of which spurted mud onto her. Stones and spreading roots and tree stumps had no effect on the speed with which they were travelling. Over obstacles and under low-hanging branches sped the bike—over and under, but never skirting an obstacle.

After what seemed to her an hour, she felt the first diminution of speed. She thought that they had reached the outskirts of the town—but Mr. Roach was merely waiting for an opportunity to slip into the stream of traffic on the main road. The going became swifter but smoother; the spurts of mud ceased. Lifting her head cautiously, she saw houses and side-turnings, and recognized the approach to the station. Then she realized that they were going on towards the road that led up the hill—he was taking her back to Lady Charlotte's house. The least he could do, she told herself; he was probably beginning to realize that he'd behaved like a savage.

His words, floating back to her, corrected this conclusion.

"Can't leave you in the middle of town, looking the

way you do," he told her. "I'm taking you up to that chap Merrion's house—that's where you're staying, isn't it?"

"No. His grandmother's," she answered, and thought that life was very varied, on the whole; who would have imagined that she would find herself on a rattletrap motorbike, clamped to a man who had insulted her after shutting her in a boot cupboard and pushing her through a window?

The bike turned in at the imposing gates. Ahead, moving at a dignified pace, was Lady Charlotte's car. Yolanda did not see it until Mr. Roach swept past it. He stopped at the foot of the steps, and Yolanda dismounted at the same moment as the big black car drew up.

There was a pause. The chauffeur came round, cap in hand, to open the door on Lady Charlotte's side and help her to alight. Getting out, she came face to face with Yolanda, and with a look of astonishment surveyed her from head to foot.

"My dear girl," she enquired frostily, "what on earth have you been up to?"

Yolanda's hair was hanging over one eye; her mackintosh, from neck to hem, was spattered with large patches of mud. Her self-assurance, however, was unimpaired.

"It was the motorbike," she began to explain. "You see, I—"

"You went out this morning with Paul, did you not?"

"That's quite right; I did. I should have taken a taxi back, but—"

"You should indeed. A hot bath, I think, and at once. Before you go, I should like to know who your friend is."

"Oh, he isn't . . ." Yolanda pulled herself up. "He's Mr. Roach."

"Then I suggest that you leave explanations to Mr. Roach, and go upstairs before you catch your death."

She turned and dismissed the car. It drove away and she was left confronting Mr. Roach.

"History master at St. Godfric's," he said. "How do you do?"

Lady Charlotte gave a slight inclination of her head. "I should like to know why Miss Purvis did not come back with Mr. Merrion."

"She must have given him the slip. The reason she didn't come back in a taxi is that there was none available. Circumstances over which I had no control necessitated my hoisting her on to the back of the bike and getting her away from the school."

"She was at the school?"

"She was."

"Why?"

"When she's had that hot bath you recommended, I daresay she'll tell you."

"Are you being impertinent?"

"Yes and no. I think my feelings are hurt because you didn't show any concern about my having a hot bath or catching my death. Not that—"

He stopped abruptly, his gaze on a gardener's boy who was pushing a wheelbarrow full of bricks across the drive. For some moments he remained motionless, staring.

"Well, will you just look at those?" he invited at last.

"At what?"

"Bricks." His eyes were following the wheelbarrow. "Beautiful, aren't they? I knew there must be some up here, of course. That is, I knew that most of them had been lifted by anybody down in the town who needed a brick or two; two hundred years is a long time. Are those all you've got left?"

"No. There are about six more wheelbarrow loads."

"What's that boy doing with them?"

"He's moving them to a safer place."

"Why? Somebody been after them?"

"Yes. Why do they interest you so much?"

"My grandfather was a builder. Early brickwork was his hobby, and he talked so much about it that it became mine. You shouldn't let that fat boy throw them into the barrow all anyhow like that. Tell him to be careful; he's handling antiques. Have you seen all the places in town where they've been used?"

"No."

"That's odd. I would have said it was the first thing you'd have been interested in finding out. I'll take you one day. There's nothing big; just pockets of them. But you'd have to go with me, because I can see you haven't an eye for brickwork, so you'd miss them. Now I'll go and see about that hot bath. Good-bye."

He made a half-circle round her, sped down the drive and slowed down to admire the statue of Hermes. Then he accelerated and was gone. She stood for a moment gazing thoughtfully after him, and then turned towards the house. Joseph, hovering patiently at the door, came down the steps to assist her. At the top, she shook off his steadying hand and issued an order.

"You may serve luncheon. We won't wait for Miss Purvis. And immediately after luncheon, I want to see the gardener."

Chapter
Six

DRYING HIMSELF AFTER HIS SHOWER on the following morning, Paul sketched out the day's programme: Down to the town with Lydia Cresset to talk to Morton at the Town Hall. And then what? He would have to do something about Yolanda Purvis. Lunch? Dinner? Either, alone with her, was a prospect too daunting to be considered for long; he would try to find someone to augment the party. This was not, he reflected bitterly, the kind of thing he had had in mind when he arranged to come to Ellstream.

His mother had finished breakfast. He ate his alone, and was walking across the hall when he heard the sound of wheels on gravel; through the circular window he saw his grandmother's car, looking almost hearse-like on this sunny morning.

He opened the front door with a slight feeling of apprehension; she had never come to the house while Esmond had occupied the guest cottage. But it was not his grandmother who got out; it was Yolanda. She thanked the chauffeur, dismissed him and told Paul she would like to speak to his mother.

"This way." He led her into the garden. "She's over at the lily pond. Know much about water lilies?"

"Quite a lot, as a matter of fact. But I can't talk about them now, because I've come to see your mother about something else. When I've talked to her, I'm going to ask you to give me a lift down to the town. I thought your grandmother would let me go in her car, but she sent a message to say I could only come here, and then I was to send the car back. I'm sure she isn't using it—she's just in a rather mean mood today. Good morning, Mrs. Merrion. I'm sorry to come so early, but I'd like to talk to you."

Mrs. Merrion, in gardening boots and gloves, smiled a greeting.

"Do you want to talk here, or inside? If you want to go in, I've finished for the moment."

But Yolanda had walked to a garden seat.

"I'm upset," she announced.

"What's upset you?" Mrs. Merrion asked. "You haven't quarrelled with Lady Charlotte, have you?"

"No, I haven't. Though quite honestly, Mrs. Merrion, I would never have come to stay with her if I'd known what a ... well, what an unsympathetic person she is. Yesterday, I almost felt like packing up and leaving. I said so to my uncle, and he said he wouldn't have minded, because it turns out that he's not at all keen on giving these lectures. I don't know why he couldn't have said so before getting me here."

"Has anything happened?" Mrs. Merrion asked.

"That's what I've come to tell you. I'll begin at the beginning. In fact"—she turned to Paul—"you were there at the beginning."

"The history master?"

114

"Yes. Mr. Roach. You heard him tell me, didn't you, that I'd ruined those library books? He said it was my fault. It wasn't, you know, but when I thought about it, I realized he might go round giving people his version and putting me in the wrong, so I decided to go up to the school and pay for the books, and that's what I did."

"I'm not sure that that was wise," Mrs. Merrion said. "But go on."

"I did it because I thought it was the right thing to do. I'm like that: I have to follow what I suppose you could call my conscience. So I went to the school intending to give him the money, but when he saw me, he was . . . well, he was terribly rude. He told me to go away, and when I said I had to send for a taxi because the one I went up in wouldn't wait, he got absolutely *livid* and shut me into a sort of cupboard while he got his ghastly motorbike, and then he rushed madly through the mud, going a long way round so's the boys wouldn't see us. When I arrived at Lady Charlotte's house, I looked a terrible sight—mud all over. All she said was that I should go and clean myself up. She didn't even wait lunch for me. At dinner last night, I told her the full story and asked her if she'd ask Mr. Roach to tea, or something, so's we could clear up this misunderstanding—but she refused to do anything, and she was very rude about my going up to the school. So I came here to ask if you could get hold of Mr. Roach. Don't you feel he owes me an apology?"

"Somehow," Paul said, "he doesn't strike me as being a man who'd know what an apology was. Don't you think it would be better to drop the whole thing?"

"No, I don't." Yolanda spoke firmly. "What do you think, Mrs. Merrion?"

"Well, perhaps it would have been better to wait and get hold of Mr. Roach after school hours, instead of going up there and interrupting him at his work. Would you like me to ask him to dinner? Tonight, if you're both free. Then you can talk the matter over in a friendly way. If I could get him to come, are you free?"

"Yes, I am. That," Yolanda said with satisfaction, "is exactly what I was hoping you'd suggest."

"Paul will go and fetch you—a quarter to eight?"

There was dismissal in her tone. Yolanda rose reluctantly.

"I've got a free morning. Are you doing anything special?" she asked Paul.

"All I'd planned was a visit to the Town Hall to see if I could fill in any more gaps in local history. If you're interested—"

"Well, frankly, *not*. The whole thing sounded to me pretty vague and speculative when we were discussing it at dinner the other night. What I think I'd rather do this morning is ride."

"Then I'll drive you over to Sir William's."

He took her there and left her. Returning, he asked his mother why she had suggested having her and Mr. Roach to dinner.

"I wasn't listening to what she said," his mother replied. "I was listening to the undertones."

"There were undertones?"

"Yes. She's longing to see him again."

"Longing to see Roach?"

"Yes."

"After he'd shut her into a cupboard and—"

"Yes."

"You're sure?"

"I'm quite sure."

"But the man's made it clear to her that all he wants is to get her out of his hair."

"He'll have to do more than shut her into a cupboard before he makes the point clear. She's a single-minded

116

young woman. She was groping for a way in which she could get in touch with him again. An apology would at least have meant confrontation."

"Who am I to argue against intuition? As we're landed with the two of them, why don't we ask Lydia Cresset and Esmond, and make it six?"

She considered.

"Yolanda would go back and tell Lottie that she'd met Esmond at my table?"

"Why not? You're free to feed him if you want to, aren't you?"

"I suppose so. Will you ask them?"

"Yes. Do you suppose I'll get anything out of this fellow Morton at the Town Hall?"

"I doubt it. There's not much on record. But his father and my father were good friends; you can give him my love."

He drove up to Mr. Ainstey's house, rang the bell and was admitted by Lydia. She led him to the kitchen, where Brenda sat drinking coffee.

"Good morning. Pour out some for him, Lydia. Home-roasted, home-ground, *specialité de la maison,*" she informed Paul. "Sit down. How is your mother?"

"She's very well, thank you. She asked me to tell you that she wishes you and Mrs. Ainstey were more neighbourly."

"By which she means we shouldn't refuse those kind invitations she sends us. But we don't visit, and that's all there is to it. We tried, long ago in London, to keep up some kind of social give-and-take, but we found there wasn't time for it. We were cooking and cleaning and looking after four growing girls. This is good coffee, isn't it?"

"It's perfect."

"That's the odd thing about people like Lydia's stepfather. They don't spread gaiety or merriment, but they keep up the standards of the people who work for them. And standards need keeping up—some standards. Food standards. This must be the only house in England which doesn't use ready-to-eat dishes."

Lydia poured herself out more coffee.

"If he had to do his own cooking," she said, "he'd reach for the can opener after the first week. Like me."

"What *do* you eat?" Brenda asked her. "You must cook something—how else would you get all that Court gossip from that Greek girl? You must spend some time in the kitchen."

"I open cans and heat the contents. And wash things for salads. And the Greek girl's very good company."

Paul finished his coffee and refused a second cup.

"If you're ready . . ." he said to Lydia.

When they were in the car, he put an unsealed envelope into her hands.

"From my mother," he said. "Formal invitation to dinner tonight, with apologies for the lack of notice. Will you come?"

"Yes. Thank you."

"Thank her—in writing, of course. Are you sure you want to waste time on Mr. Morton?"

"Yes."

They walked into the Town Hall to be informed that Mr. Morton was out, but would be back in twenty minutes, if they cared to wait. Paul led Lydia out again.

"No need to wait," he said. "Anybody who's going to be back in twenty minutes is obviously having a quick one in the nearest pub."

Mr. Morton was not in the nearest pub, but in the Plough, two streets away. Going in, they asked for him and were directed to a small table in a warm corner of the room. Paul, introducing Lydia and himself, was about to

118

suggest a move to a sunny bench in the window, when it struck him that perhaps Mr. Morton would prefer to remain out of sight of inquisitive passersby who might wonder why he was not at work.

He was drinking cider, which he informed them was as good here as in Devonshire. Paul ordered three glasses and brought chairs. Mr. Morton, middle-aged, almost bald, with brown button eyes in a round, red face, asked permission to go on smoking his pipe.

"It's the only place I can enjoy it," he said. "My wife has jumped on no fewer than seven expensive pipes. I hide 'em, but she goes on looking and in the end she finds 'em. You didn't need to tell me who you were," he informed Paul. "You've been pointed out to me several times when you've come on one of your flying visits. Funny, your mother coming back to her birthplace to settle. Did she tell you that her father and mine were friends?"

"She did, and she sent her love."

"The same to her. She's often asked my wife and m'self to this and that, but my wife's not easy to move; before she'll go visiting, she has to have her hair done and her dresses let down or taken up, and she finds her shoes aren't what they're wearing this year, and by the time she's got herself sorted, she's changed her mind about going. What did you want to see me about?"

"Local history," said Paul.

Mr. Morton pushed away his empty glass and reached for the full one that had been set before him.

"Your good health," he said. "Local history? Your mother's family history?"

"No. Just some facts about the houses that stood on the hill my grandmother built her house on."

"Splendid house she put up," Mr. Morton commented. "A lot of us down here thought she was overdoing it. In fact, there was a kind of movement to point out to her the error of her ways. The parson wanted money for his church, the school would have liked some, even the Scouts and the Guides and half a dozen other organizations held out their hats. The church ladies said it was disgraceful to build a mansion when there were people starving all over the world. But nobody got as far as tackling your grandmother, and once the place was built, it was voted a building we could all be proud of, instead of that mouldering old ruin. There are ruins and ruins; some are picturesque, but that one wasn't. Who told you to come and ask me about local history?"

"Miss Clarendon."

"Ah. Whispering Winnie. Did she tell you to hush?"

"Yes."

"Anything else?"

"She showed us a print of the ruin and told us the house had been built in 1756. And I know there was an earlier house on the site."

"Yes. Tudor. 1520. The one your grandmother pulled down was built by a chap who was in the East India Company. That's to say, it was built by his wife, if she was his wife. The job owed nothing to the local professionals. The architect and the plans, in fact the whole project was hatched in London. All the wife had to do was watch the building going up. The brick tower seems to have been her own idea, and it was a good one; she must have thought it a pity to waste all those nice old bricks. This is wonderful cider, isn't it?"

"Yes. Do they sell it in bottles?" Lydia asked.

"No. There's only a limited supply. It comes in barrels from a farm about three miles upriver. My wife and I keep trying to get them to produce more of it, but they won't; they've got enough for themselves, and a bit over, and that satisfies them."

"About this wife—" Paul began.

Mr. Morton brought his attention reluctantly from cider to the subject under discussion.

"Well, what about her?" he asked.

"It's curious that nobody seems to know anything about her. If you consider what an out-of-the-way place this must have been in those days, and if you imagine the effect of planting an Indian princess in the middle of the yokels, wouldn't you think there would have been a lot of gossip at the time, and a number of legends in our time?"

"That's something that's always puzzled me, too. But it's doubtful that she was a princess, and it's even doubtful that she was this chap Exerton's wife. It's probable that she kept herself to herself. Certainly nothing's known about her except that she gave orders for the bricks from the old Tudor house to be used for the tower."

"She died here, didn't she?"

"Yes. But she wasn't buried here. Pity she didn't live a bit longer—but even if she had, she wouldn't have seen Exerton, because he ended up in the river, before he'd even set eyes on his house."

"Would you say that the reason nothing much was known was because Exerton didn't want it known? Those East India Company fellows had plenty of opportunity for making big hauls. Could there have been anything fishy behind it? His wife might have been told to keep herself to herself."

Mr. Morton studied him across the little round oak table.

"You've really got your teeth into it, haven't you?" he remarked.

"Not at the start. But I find that the more one gropes, the less there is to hold on to. East India Company, Indian princess, a house going up, a tower going up—and scarcely one item of information available about that couple. They presumably meant to settle here, didn't they?"

"I daresay. I'm sorry I can't help you more. There's nothing in the records. Your grandfather—your mother's father—went to a lot of trouble to try and find out something definite, but—"

"All guesswork. I know."

"You'd really like to go on digging?"

"While I'm here, yes. I'm not here for long."

"Well, there's one thread you could follow. I suppose you know that the family of that coachman who was killed when the coach went into the river, came and settled here?"

"Yes."

"Well, go and see them. Your grandfather would have liked to have a chat, but in his day there was an old beldame who used to set the dogs on anybody that wasn't on farm business. She's dead, and maybe the dogs are dead too. The name's Darsett. They've done well since they settled here. They started in a hovel on three acres of land, and went on to . . . well, you'll see. There's an old man, son of the old beldame, but he doesn't do much but sleep; the farm's run by the grandson, John Darsett. He often comes into town—he's a decent fellow."

"Where's the farm?"

"Near a village called Rawley, about eight miles down the river. It's more a hamlet than a village, and most of it, and the land round it, belongs to the Darsetts. Then if you get nothing out of them, you might try old Mrs. Meader."

"Who's she?"

"Going on for ninety, living in a house in which her forebears have lived since the beginning of time. She could have been a source—she once told my father she had some interesting old letters, but he could never get a look at them because she could never remember where she'd put them. She might know now, because for the past couple of years, she's been looked after by a sensible niece.

Go and try your luck. Her house is two miles beyond Rawley, visible from the road—you can't miss it." He rose. "Work calls. Thanks for the drink. Tell your mother we'll be up one of these days to pay her a visit."

They walked back with him to the Town Hall and left him there. Then Paul looked at his watch.

"No time to get out to Rawley and back before lunch," he said. "How about this afternoon?"

She hesitated, and he spoke again.

"Lost interest?"

"No."

"Then what's the objection to doing a bit more research? Is there anything else one can do to fill in time in this place?"

"You came to see your mother. Maybe she'd like—"

"Correction. I came here so that my fiancée could meet my mother. Until she comes back from Venice, I've got time on my hands. Let's call it an interregnum. So as you and I both have time on our hands, this method of using it is more interesting than most. Will you come?"

"Yes. Thank you."

She saw him smile, and asked what was amusing him.

"Your way of saying yes, and following it up with a thank you, giving it a grudging sound. Did they have a job making you say thank you when you were a child? As we're proceeding with our investigation this afternoon," he went on, "the most sensible thing would be to have lunch together. Between here and Rawley there's a place we could eat. Want to try it? It's a cross between a pub and a farmhouse. Plain fare, vast helpings. With luck, we might get them to produce some of Mr. Morton's brand of cider. After which we'd call on the Darsetts. After which we'll drop in on my uncle to invite him to dinner. After which I'll go up to the school—alone—to try and induce our friend Roach to make one of the party."

123

"Induce?"

"Once he hears that Yolanda's to be in the party, he'll need persuading. Apart from that, did he strike you as being a social animal?"

"Couldn't tell. He was unloading a grievance. But if he's going to be in the party, won't Yolanda want persuading too?"

"According to my mother, she'd rather like to see him again. Do you want to phone your aunt before we get too far out of town, to tell her you won't be back for lunch?"

They stopped at an A.A. box, and Lydia made the call. When she was back in the car, Paul asked a question.

"How long has your mother been married to your stepfather?"

"Four years. But she knew him for about ten years before that, when he lived in our house in London. When my father died, she decided to keep on the house, but couldn't afford to unless she took in paying guests. There were three rooms and Mr. Ainstey took them all, and it worked well—he liked comfort and she provided it. That's been her sole occupation ever since she left school—making a man comfortable. First her father, then my father and after him my stepfather. She never had any servants—the reason my aunt was needed was because there had to be a set of separate meals for the lodger. Then when he retired and built this house, they got married and came to Ellstream. My sisters were against it."

"But not you?"

"No. I didn't like him, but I could see they'd make a good pair, he and my mother. If she hadn't married him, she wouldn't have had a home, because the one we lived in wasn't ours, and was going to be sold. So they got married. My sisters were teaching, and married or going to be. I was eighteen, and living in a hostel for music students. It was only when I left it that I realized I hadn't got a home. Staying with my stepfather didn't work—so I got myself a bed-sitter, and settled down. It's not bad; I keep plants in the so-called garden outside, and I keep my bike down there so's nobody'll walk off with it when I'm not using it."

Silence fell. He was following the course of her life and wondering what there had been in it to leave her with this air of serenity. She was one of the most completely relaxed women he had ever met; she might have been called dull, he thought, but for two things: the musical quality of her voice, which made a listener follow with interest everything she said—and the humour, the quiet sense of fun that could be seen in her eyes. She had a bed-sitter and a bicycle, and she was happy. He had . . . God, what had he not had all his life? Luxurious homes, money, Cambridge, travel, friends, sport, women—and for the past year, he had not known what the word happiness meant. And now he was stranded, and if Diana Framley came back to him, he would be caught by the tide and dragged back into turbulent waters, to try and keep afloat, as he had tried throughout his association with her.

Beside him, Lydia let him dream. She did not think they were pleasant dreams, and longed to ask him what was wrong. As she couldn't, she would have to make the most of whatever pleasure she could get by helping him to fill in time. When she got back to London, she might learn from the Greek girl what had happened—or perhaps not, since Diana Framley was using Venetian hairdressers.

When they stopped for lunch, she found that he had not overstated the liberality of the farmhouse fare. They sat in the huge kitchen beside the open range, at the end of a table along which were ranged the farmer and his family and his farm hands. His wife and two daughters ladled food from steaming containers onto plates, carried them to the table and then sat down to eat. There were second and third helpings—thick slices of beef, batter pudding swimming in gravy, baked potatoes; cabbage, carrots and turnips all served in the same dish, and apple dumplings and cheese. There was no cider; they drank beer from pewter tankards and wiped the foam from their lips on coarse linen napkins. They were not offered coffee at the end of the meal, but a gigantic teapot was set in front of the hostess, flanked by a large jug of milk and a pudding basin filled with sugar. The price, Paul said, putting away his change and leading Lydia out to the car, would have paid for the rolls and butter provided with the meal in a less humble restaurant.

"I've eaten too much," he stated. "I don't think I'm going to fit between the seat and the driving wheel." He opened the car doors. "I don't suppose . . ." He stopped, staring at her. *"Still* eating?" he asked in stupefied tones.

"She gave me an apple while you were paying the bill. Lovely and juicy."

"Would you like me to look the other way while you loosen your girdle?"

"No girdle."

"Doesn't your aunt feed you properly?"

"Yes. But I like filling in."

"You mean filling up."

"I've decided," she said, as he started the car, "that I'd like to marry a farmer."

"Just for the food?"

"And the nice, open-air life."

"I don't suppose that farmer's wife enjoyed much open-air life while she was cooking all that stuff."

"A man I know, a violinist, went off about two months ago, with a rucksack and his violin and no money, and he's playing his way round Europe."

"They pay him to go and perform somewhere else?"

"No. He's a good violinist."

"It's not a good solo instrument, in my opinion. Why didn't he take an accordion or a guitar? He could play the accordion for the folk dancing, and he could serenade the girls with his guitar. But sawing away at a violin with your hat on the pavement in front of you—that isn't the way to do it."

"I'll remember that. Thank you."

"You're thinking of following your friend?"

"I'll wait and see if the quartet gets together again. Can you play the piano or the cello or anything?"

"The recorder, when I was eight. It was my first year at my prep school, and I played a recorder duet with another unfortunate. We both forgot the notes. He didn't even finish—he walked off the platform and I was left playing the tuneless second part. That was my last appearance on any stage and my last attempt to master an instrument. Was that the Rawley sign I just passed?"

"Yes. I suppose your chauffeur nudges you when you're getting near the turning?"

"If he nudged me, he'd be out of a job. Can you remember why we're going to Rawley?"

"Yes. To see the Darsetts."

"Can you by any chance remember why?"

"To ask them why their ancestors came here two hundred years ago."

"Seems an odd kind of question to throw at a farmer on a busy afternoon. Old Morton was right; they've prospered. Nice spread." He stopped the car to study it. "Dairy cattle. And crops. How do you suggest we account for our sudden interest in his ancestors?"

"*Your* sudden interest."

"You said—"

"I want to see what you find out, if anything. And it's better to have two people to sift the findings."

"You're a big help." He drove towards the farmhouse.

"The nearer we get, the more I understand why my grandmother wrote it off as guesswork."

To right and left were fields on which Friesians grazed. He reached the rambling old house and stopped at the front door. Getting out, he looked for a knocker or a bell rope, found none and used his fist. There was no response.

"Good. All out," he announced, returning to the car. "Expedition a total failure. Let's go."

"Why? There's bound to be somebody at home. Let's try round the back."

"You try."

"You mean you'd just give up and drive away?"

"With the utmost relief. It's all very well to sit round a table discussing this kind of thing, but when you set out on imaginary trails, where do you get?"

"We've got to where you wanted to get, so it's silly to leave without talking to somebody. Come round the back."

As she stepped out of the car, the front door opened. From the house came a child of about six, a kitten under each arm. She gave the visitors a frowning look.

"You waked up Grandad," she informed them. "He's steaming."

"I'm sorry about that," Paul said. "Is your father in?"

"No. Dad's with the tractor in the ten-acre. Tommy's in the turnip field. Ern's gone carting stuff over to Barney's place. Frank's mending the roof of the cowshed. Mum's in the kitchen shelling peas. I'm going to call my kittens Dizzy and Tizzy. My name's Vanessa. I go to school, but not today because I've got a bad cold."

This was only too evident. Paul turned to Lydia.

"Your choice," he said. "Dad? It looks like a long walk. Tommy, Frank, Ern or Mum?"

"Dad. If the tractor got there, couldn't the car?"

"The tractor crosses fields. Don't you like walking?"

"No."

"It's less tiring than all that bicycling you do, isn't it?"

"No. On a bicycle, you're sitting down. But if I have to walk, I have to. Let's go."

"I'll take you," Vanessa offered. "I know the way to go."

"No. You'd make your cold worse in those damp fields," Paul told her. "We'll find the way."

Without arguing, she went into the house and closed the door. Paul and Lydia set off in the direction of the tractor to be seen three fields away. Halfway across the first, they wished they had accepted Vanessa's offer to guide them.

"The ends of my trousers are soaking, and so are yours," Paul said. "We'll soon be sniffing like Vanessa. Can you negotiate that stile? If not, I'll haul you over it, which is more than I could do for Yolanda."

They negotiated two stiles.

"My enthusiasm," he said, "was never great. Now it's nonexistent. Let's go back."

"Too late. He's seen us."

The farmer, at the far corner of the field, raised a hand and continued his journey until it brought him close to them. Then he stopped the tractor, stepped down and joined them.

"Good afternoon. Want to see me?" he asked.

"You're Mr. Darsett?"

"Right. You shouldn't have come across the fields. There's a dry way round 'em that young Vanessa could've shown you, if she'd had a mind."

"She offered," Lydia said.

"And you said you'd manage. Town folk," guessed Mr. Darsett. "What can I do for you?"

"This lady," Paul said, "is Miss Cresset, a reporter on a London paper. She's spending a short time in Ellstream and she heard about the connection your family has with the coach incident in Ellstream, and asked me to bring her out to see you. My name's Merrion. My—"

"Ah. Your grandma built that great house up there, didn't she?"

"Yes. Miss Cresset was interested to hear the story of the house that was built on the site before my grandmother inherited the land. So I brought her along to talk to you, to see if you could tell her anything about the coachman who died in the accident. He was a Darsett, wasn't he?"

"Right. London man, he was. We don't know nothin' about him, except that he come from a big family, but he was the only one to pull up stakes and decide to settle here. But he didn't settle; he was drowned and so was one of his sons, later on. There's a lot of talk about why he came, but there's nothing in it. Treasure, they said. If there'd been any treasure around, he wouldn't have left his widow and family to set up in a hovel in the middle of a field, like this was once. You see, Miss, rumours get flying round, and you can't tell where they'll finish up."

"Miss Cresset hoped there might be some family history, or some legends, that you might be able to tell her."

Mr. Darsett shook his head.

"Nothing to tell," he answered. "You're not the first that's been round asking, though you're the first for a long time. My old grandma used to chase people away, set the dogs on 'em. Maybe she could have showed 'em that bit of paper we found in her room, but there wasn't nothing much on it to show, and if there had been, she wouldn't have shown it."

"What paper?" Lydia asked.

"It won't help you much, but you can go back to the house and ask my missus and she'll show it to you. It was in an old cupboard my Grandma picked up at a sale. She was always one for going to sales—she said that furniture must know secrets. There must be a lot of furniture in these farmhouses that came from the old stone house that was up on the hill. Stands to reason, doesn't it? It was full of furniture, and nobody ever lived there, and nobody took the furniture away. My Grandma had an eye for good old stuff. She used to make a bit of money buying and selling."

"What was on the paper?" Lydia asked.

"If you can make it out, you'll be cleverer than all of us, Miss. It's a bit of an old newspaper. It was young Ern who said I shouldn't throw it away. My wife's got it, for what it's worth. Go up and ask her, and she'll show it to you."

"Thank you. I'm sorry we interrupted your work."

"You're welcome any time," Mr. Darsett declared. "I didn't stop the tractor. Every time it sees a lovely young lady like you, it stops itself."

On this pleasant note they parted, Mr. Darsett pointing out the dry route back to the farmhouse.

"What paper do I report for?" Lydia asked when they had left the farmer behind.

"Take your choice. Left wing, right wing?"

"Left. I suppose you're extreme right?"

"I'm extreme nothing. I'm middle-of-the-road. If this bit of newssheet was in a piece of furniture which belonged to the man who built the house which . . . I'm getting confused."

"What I can't understand is how a piece of paper could last two hundred years—if it's as old as that. A sheet of newspaper—"

"It wouldn't have been made out of wood pulp, like the paper you work for. It was only between 1840 and 1866 that they began to use wood pulp."

"So if it isn't made out of wood pulp, what'll it be made out of?"

"Cotton and linen rags, moistened, fermented, washed and pulped. Would you like me to enlarge on the methods of manufacture?"

"Could you?"

He put out a hand to prevent her from slipping off the narrow ledge along which they were walking.

"I could talk for an hour. I gave a lecture on the subject to the staff at the Bank."

"A lecture on newspapers?"

"No. On paper-making. Bankers deal in banknotes, among other things, and I thought the younger members of the staff ought to know at least something about the paper on which banknotes are printed. Didn't your school ever take parties of you round printing works?"

"No. How long ago did newspapers start?"

"When man started. I read somewhere that man has always needed his newspaper, in some form or other. There are no human beings—it's said—so primitive as to be uninterested in their own or their neighbours' affairs. I'd question that myself, but I'm willing to learn. You had drums and then you had the bush telegraph and hieroglyphics carved by the first reporters on rock or stone and later on metal slabs or clay tablets or waxed boards or papyrus or parchment. The first paper appeared about a hundred years after Christ appeared, but the process was kept secret by the Chinese for hundreds of years. Then round about the eighth century, some unfortunate Chinese papermakers were caught by the Moors and the secret got out. We go on to newsletters and postboys and couriers and to the telegraph. Have you heard enough about newspapers?"

"No. Go on."

"Most instructors make a charge. What we're going to be shown will probably be a fragment of an old newssheet. The *London Gazette* appeared in 1666 and has been appearing twice a week ever since. Are we going to knock on the front door again?"

"No. The back, this time."

Vanessa opened the door, still holding the kittens. Behind her, seated at a long trestle table, was a middle-aged woman, plump and pink-cheeked, her hands dealing swiftly and efficiently with a sack still half full of peas. The motions of grasping several pods from the sack, splitting them and thumbing the peas into a large earthenware bowl on the table, were so smooth and continuous as to look like the working of a machine.

"Come in, come on in," she called. "I heard you knocking before, but I couldn't stop."

Paul followed Lydia into the warm kitchen.

"I'm told we woke Vanessa's grandfather," he said.

"You did. He'll get over it. Did you see her Dad?"

"Yes. My name's Paul Merrion. This is Miss Cresset, a reporter on a London paper. She's only here for a short time, but she wanted to find out something about that old accident to the coach—it's the only bit of local history we can offer her. Your husband said there was a bit of paper—"

"There's nothing on it you can read. We'd have thrown it out if it hadn't been for Ern saying it was so old. Vanessa, fetch it."

Vanessa put the kittens on the table, dragged a chair to the high cupboard in a corner, opened the doors, clambered on to the chair and from the back of a shelf lifted a book.

"I put it in a book to keep it flat," Mrs. Darsett explained. "It was Ern wouldn't let us throw it away—did Mr. Darsett tell you? You won't see much writing on it."

There was even less than Paul had expected to see. The paper was thick, yellow with age, and had at some time been wet, so that reading the print was a matter of deciphering four or five badly smudged lines. He and Lydia studied it together.

"Not much, is there?" Mrs. Darsett commented. "If it had a date, that would've been something to help."

"Would you let Miss Cresset make a note of what there is?"

"Help yourself," said Mrs. Darsett, still mechanically shelling peas. "Pen on the mantelpiece if you want one."

"I've got my own; thanks," Lydia said, and copied into Paul's diary as much as she could decipher of the print.

"There'll be a hot cup of tea ready soon, if you'll wait," Mrs. Darsett offered. "Nice hot scones with it, if you're not worried about weight, like most are nowadays. I've got to get these peas ready for the deep-freeze, but I won't be long now."

"That's very kind, but we have to go," Lydia said.

They thanked her and made their farewells. Vanessa, picking up the kittens, accompanied the visitors to the door.

In the car, they reviewed the visit.

"Still want to be a farmer's wife?" Paul asked.

"Maybe not. There's a bit too much open air. And I suppose London's got into my blood—born in London, educated in London, living in London, working in London except when we can't get engagements there and have to play in the provinces. Sometimes I feel it would be nice if they could move out five or six million and make more room for the rest, but I don't really mind being one of the crowd. When you come to think of it, what is there to do anywhere that you can't do in London?"

"Ski?"

"If you've never been on skis, you don't miss them. I've tobogganed down Camden Hill."

"What do you do in your spare time?"

"When I'm not busy reporting? Oh, shows, films, concerts, picture galleries, even museums in the worst of the winter—they're nice and warm. When the quartet's done a longer spell than usual out of London, I'm always glad to get back. If you'll stop the car for a minute, I'd like to take another look at what was on that piece of paper."

He stopped the car down a side-turning, and handed her his diary. As at the farm, they studied the sparse letters together.

"Nothing," Paul summed up at last. "Not a single date, not a single clue."

"If it's true—which it is—that there must be a lot of furniture in these surrounding farmhouses that used to be in that house belonging to the man called Exerton, then it's probable that the paper was once in his house. You agree?"

"I'll go as far as to agree that if anybody was interested in reading the newssheets, it would be someone in the Exerton educational bracket. He could have sent them to his wife. Or she could have got hold of them herself. Next point?"

"She couldn't have read any after she was dead, so if the paper was in that house, it must have been there at about the time we're trying to fill in. Right?"

"No comment. Proceed."

"So let's say that this paper was a piece of a newssheet printed during the building of the house. Having said that, you take another look and what do you see?"

"Nothing of any interest."

"That's because you're not a reporter. Take another look. Can you see those three letters, the end of a word ending in *-ton?* Well, Exerton ends *-ton.*"

"And so?"

"So you go on, and you see that there's a word that's quite clear: confinement. It can't mean that Exerton had a baby, so why can't it mean prison? If you accept that,

and I know it's hard to swallow, then those other letters
—look—can be the end of the word released."

"Ah. They let him out?"

"Why not? He was in that coach, wasn't he?"

"Go on."

"This word here—it's smudged, but I'm certain it's
Company with a capital C. If it is, then I submit that
what the paper said was that Mr. Exerton, late of the East
India Company, had been released from prison."

"One of my grandmother's connections—however distant—in jug?"

"Why should that surprise you? Didn't most of those
earls and barons have doubtful records? Since this has
been guesswork from the start, we can at least try to make
the guesses fit—and this fits all the way round. The wife,
or mistress, is sent by Exerton to Ellstream to superintend
the building of the house. He can't accompany her because he's unfortunately been thrown into prison. You
said yourself that he had some connection with Warren
Hastings, who—"

"All I said—"

"—was impeached for something or other. They
wouldn't impeach a minor official like Exerton; they'd
just imprison him, wouldn't they? News like that leaks
out and in the end reaches places even as small and as
remote as Ellstream must have been in those days. There
was a name for people, Europeans, who got rich rather
fast in the East—what was it?"

"Nabob."

"That's it, nabob. So a thread of rumour hangs from
those facts—a nabob returned from India and thrown into
prison and then released, and shortly afterwards travelling with his hoard in a coach to join his girl friend. Do
you wonder people got drowned looking for treasure?"

"No."

"But you don't agree with one word of the theory?"

"I'm fascinated. I never knew before how the minds of reporters worked. Out of three guesses, a reconstruction."

"It could be near the truth, couldn't it?"

"It could. Nobody's in a position to dispute it. So as we know the entire story, why are we driving to see old Mrs. Meader, whose memory is faulty but who keeps letters?"

"We might get something else to work on."

"We're working?"

"I am. I'm a reporter, remember?"

"Then will you start thinking of some good opening remarks to address to the old lady?"

They were not needed. Paul's car drove up behind the doctor's. The doctor, coming a few steps towards them, asked if they were relatives; on being informed that they were not even acquainted with Mrs. Meader, he broke the news: she was sinking fast and quite unable to receive anybody. There was nothing to do but drive away.

"I would have liked to have seen her," Lydia said thoughtfully on the way back to Ellstream. "I've never seen anybody as old as that, and I'd imagined her as a spry old lady sitting in a high-backed chair looking over her collection of letters and burning some of them in case they fell into the wrong hands. I hope she gets better."

"At that age, would you want to?"

"If I'd got so far, I'd like to make it a hundred."

"I don't think I want to get as far. Are you coming with me to see Esmond?"

"I'd rather go straight home, please. Will you ask him to wait for me tonight? I'll go over to the cottage and he and I can walk up to your house together."

He drove her to Mr. Ainstey's house. As they reached the gate, Paul had to slow down to allow a car to come out. He gave an exclamation of astonishment.

"Lottie's car—without Lottie." He stopped his car and

lowered the window to address the chauffeur as the black car came alongside. "Have you left her ladyship in the house?"

"No, sir. I brought a letter for Mr. Ainstey."

"I see."

"Letter?" Lydia repeated as they drove on. "He and she aren't friends, are they? Don't go away. I've got a feeling this might mean trouble."

Brenda let them in. Behind her, at the door of his study, they saw Mr. Ainstey with an opened letter in his hand. He was standing motionless, looking down at it with a dazed expression. Then he raised his head. A violent flush spread over his cheeks and seemed to swell them. His eyes glared unseeingly at the two who had just entered the hall. He made an attempt to speak, failed to utter anything coherent, and with a gesture of fury, went into his study and banged the door. Lydia, her eyes wide with wonder, looked at Brenda.

"What's wrong?" she whispered.

Brenda spoke in a low voice.

"Remember those bricks of Lady Charlotte's he helped himself to?"

"Yes."

"I saw him open the letter. Inside it was a bill for the bricks."

Chapter Seven

DUDLEY ROACH ENTERED the history classroom on the stroke of three o'clock. At his entrance, the sixteen boys awaiting him sprang to their desks and stood at attention. There was total silence as he stepped up on to the dais and faced the class. It was not the silence of fear, but the silence of respect—and he felt that he had earned it. This was his sixth year of teaching history, and his third term at St. Godric's, and his reputation was that of a master able to produce order from the kind of chaos that only small boys can create.

His first appearance in a class at St. Godric's had made school history. The class—the oldest boys in the school—was in his opinion far too large: he had told himself that twenty-two of the little bastards, all hell-bent on wrecking the efforts of any master to drive knowledge into their heads, was about ten too many. His first act would be to reduce the size of the classes.

The class had begun with Mr. Roach as it meant to go

on: chattering, cuffing one another and affecting deafness when requested to desist. Suddenly Mr. Roach advanced upon the four ringleaders and, carrying them to the window two by two, tossed them out on to the petunia beds eight feet below. As the second pair vanished, he faced the class, his expression one of hope. But there were no more takers. To protesting parents—who received merely token support from the Headmaster—Mr. Roach pointed out that the day had been a rainy one, the flower beds were muddy and the ground soft and yielding; the victims, landing face down, had risen looking no dirtier than they looked when coming off the rugger field. After this incident, his talent for teaching was exercised in ideal conditions.

He began today as he always began; the boys would have felt themselves cheated if he had varied the introduction in any particular. From the dais, looking as mighty as Jove, he gave his pupils a polite bow.

"Good afternoon, gentlemen."

"Good afternoon, sir."

"I trust you lunched well, and enjoyed some fresh air after your meal."

"Yes, thank you, sir."

"Then pray be seated. Before we resume our researches into the life and achievements of Alexander the Great, I would like to point out the mistake that almost all of you made in stating that he lived two thousand years ago. If you will add the present year to the years before Christ, you will get the right number. Don't let B.C. dates confuse you. Incidentally, as we have touched on the birth of Christ, I would like to tell Eldridge and Allen, who were discussing the event in the corridor this morning as I passed, that their views on the matter are far from accurate. I have asked the biology master to give them a brief refresher course on the topic. Now we shall look at the death of Darius."

Discussing Darius, Dudley let a part of his mind review his own life plan. A school of his own. Not when he was middle-aged; a school of his own soon. A small school —about sixty boys to start with. No girls. From a family point of view, coeducation was all right, but his teaching methods, he felt, were more successful with boys than they would be with a mixed class. A place in the country, but not one large building; two or three moderate-sized ones, to avoid the institutional look that had oppressed him when he arrived at his prep school. Money? He had some, and his sister wanted to come in with the packet her husband had left her. Staff? All in good time. A fine life, if he could bring it off—doing the thing he liked best, and doing it not only for his own pleasure but for his own profit.

There were two classes after the one he was teaching now. It was a quarter past five when he was free. He went to the gymnasium as usual to correct exercise books, but he did not settle down to work as readily as he usually did; the thought that that girl might appear at any moment and try to push some more money at him was a disturbing one. What a name: Yolanda. It could be an au pair girl or a Swiss cow. She was sparsely furnished as regards brain, but those muscular girls usually were. There was something in that brawn versus brain theory. You could see it in these boys: the oversized chaps walked off with the sports trophies, but the weedy ones could be counted on to march off with the scholarships. The theory didn't hold water in his own case—he had been a heavyweight all his life, but he had never wanted to be on a games field if he could be at his desk or in a library.

The correcting finished, he opened his notebook to jot

down the outline of tomorrow's lessons. Intent on what he was doing, the thump on the door brought him upright in his chair with a start. If it was that girl again, he told himself, he would haul her bodily to the Headmaster and ... no, he couldn't risk it. If one of those dirty-minded young boys caught sight of him with a girl on the school premises, he could write off any authority he'd gained over them.

He walked across the room and opened the door. On the threshold, to his relief, was not a girl, but a man: Paul Merrion.

"Oh, hello," he said. "Come in."

Paul hesitated.

"If I'm interrupting, or if I've chosen a bad time, or if visits—"

"I'm free. Come in." He closed the door behind Paul and went straight to the point. "This anything to do with the Purvis girl?"

"Yes." Paul looked round for something to sit on. "Can I bring that bench nearer?"

Dudley dragged it closer and sat at one end.

"Expound," he invited.

"Yolanda came to see my mother this morning."

"And your mother sent you here to tell me I was to go to the Headmaster's study for six of the best?"

"No. To ask you, if you're free this evening, to come and dine with us, short notice notwithstanding."

"There's a catch somewhere. That girl's going to be there too?"

"Yes. The idea is to get the two of you together to make peace."

"Peace? Would you accept an invitation to sit at a dinner table with a woman who did what she did to me, to you?"

"Why not? The point is, she's my grandmother's guest and we wouldn't like her to go away with a grievance."

Dudley stood up.

"Grievance? *Grievance?*" He glared down at Paul. "Look, camarade, it's obvious that I didn't make myself clear when confronted by the Purvis outside the library. The sight of her probably made me garble the story. But the facts are incontrovertible. She ousted those Scouts, my Scouts, from a field they were occupying with the owner's permission. Her story is that she didn't know they were there, but do you buy that? I don't. Whoever she gave her orders to must have told her that the Scouts were encamped."

"Not necessarily. She gave the order to somebody down at the stables. There was a breakdown in communication, that's all."

"That's not all, but there's nothing to be gained by arguing. If she'd known the Scouts were there, would she have cared? No. You've only got to look at her: stuffed with self-sufficiency, living in a world of horses and disregarding anything on two legs instead of four. She's one of those people who turn on-the-fencers into Communists overnight. I thought we'd had a social revolution that sent all the over-privileged rolling to oblivion in tumbrils, but you still get pockets of them here and there, and this girl's one of them. I don't like her. I don't like her name or her voice or her manner. I don't like being addressed in that take-your-hat-off-when-I-speak-to-you tone. Does she know about this get-together tonight?"

"My mother told her she'd try and arrange it."

"I'm surprised to find that I come up to the Purvis's level of what she'd call acceptability. Plain Roach, I am, grandson of a builder, son of a small-town solicitor and a subscriber to every leftish paper in circulation. If the idea

143

behind this invitation is to wring an apology out of me, tell your mother with my thanks and compliments that it's not on."

"I will. But it would be nice if you came, and came early so that we could have a quiet drink before the others turn up."

"What others?"

"Lydia Cresset—the girl who was present when you made your speech outside the library—and my uncle, Esmond Merrion."

"Is he the chap that's got a reputation for wheedling the local tradesmen into letting him have goods he can't pay for?"

"The same. How do these things get known? He's only been to Ellstream once before, and that was years ago. He reappeared without notice two days ago, and as far as I know, he's only been into town twice since he came. So how—"

"This is a small town and a dull town. Is he really the crook he's reported to be?"

"Come to dinner and ask him."

"He sounds to me like a rebel of some sort—probably in revolt against the rest of his family, stinking rich bankers with two or three cars apiece and a private plane and lots of chums in very high places. Why can't this dinner be for your uncle without the Purvis?"

"We'll put you at one end of the table and Yolanda at the other."

"Her voice carries. How do you know I won't give her further cause to complain?"

"You'd find it difficult in my mother's house."

"Oh, calming influence?"

"Haven't you ever seen her?"

"No. Is she anything like your grandmother?"

"Entirely different species. Coming?"

"Yes. Don't run away with the idea that you've persuaded me."

"I won't. As I said, come early."

"What was the version Yolanda Purvis gave your mother?"

"You shut her in a cupboard and then put her on a dangerous machine and roared through the mud to my grandmother's."

"Have you any idea what would have happened if any of the boys had seen her making her way to a place which, I'd made clear, was at certain hours to be my own private domain?"

"I can guess." He rose. "Well, until later."

"I suppose, as you're here, you wouldn't care to be shown round the school?"

"No, thanks. I don't mind putting my sons' names down on the waiting list, if you'd like me to."

"Not on this waiting list. I'm going to have a prep school of my own."

"You'd accept the sons of stinking rich bankers?"

"Must get a start somehow. Do I have to change tonight?"

"No."

"Then thank your mother for her kind invitation and tell her I have much pleasure in accepting. See what a big swindle it all is, this social stuff? She's being kind to the Purvis, not to me, and the only pleasure I'll have is in meeting your disreputable uncle."

He took Paul's advice and arrived early. In the drawing room, comfortable in a deep chair, drink in hand, he talked to Mrs. Merrion of schools past and present.

"You need time to build up a sound reputation," he said. "But you don't need a lifetime. This school here isn't long-established as schools go—a hundred years or so—but in that time, it's climbed right to the top of the prep school class."

"My father was one of the early pupils," she said. "There were only two buildings then. He built the wing they named after him."

"The Provost wing?"

"Yes."

"Your father?"

"Yes. Didn't you know I was born in this town?"

"I may have heard that, but I didn't know you were the daughter of Provost. He built the big gymnasium, too."

"And the cricket pavilion and the indoor swimming pool, and later the outdoor one. There wasn't much money when the school started; most of it came from benefactors. Now it's well on its feet. Paul tells me you hope to start a school of your own."

"Not hope; intend. I've been saving for years and wringing donations out of any relations who had any dough to spare. I call the fund the Dudley Roach Foundation."

"You like teaching?"

"Yes. But it wasn't the urge to teach that started me off. I spent my prep-school years trying to learn in classes no master ever seemed able to control. Riots all through the sessions. I suppose I was as bad as the rest, but I always knew where the unfortunate master went wrong, and I knew that in his place, I would have been able to get the little devils under control and create conditions in which those who wanted to learn, could learn."

Paul, watching the two, saw that they liked one another and were enjoying themselves—so much so that it was with reluctance that they broke off their conversation and rose at the entry of Lydia and Esmond. Paul drove across to fetch Yolanda; when she entered the room, she was wearing a long, clinging dress—the only person in the room in formal clothes.

"You told me not to change," she said to Mrs. Merrion as she came in, "but it's a sort of habit I've got—I just *have* to get into something pretty in the evenings."

Lydia, in a trouser suit, thought the dress anything but pretty, but it looked expensive. It was also, like Yolanda's other clothes, outmoded. But if you spent most of your time in a riding outfit, perhaps you didn't have time to notice what fashion was doing.

There was no awkwardness about the meeting between Yolanda and Dudley. Her speech was obviously rehearsed, and she made it in a loud voice and with considerable heartiness.

"Do you mind if I call you Dudley? I can't bear being addressed as Miss Purvis, so it'll have to be Yolanda and Dudley, if you don't mind. I've got a message for you from Lady Charlotte—she says that any time you want to go up and look at bricks, you're welcome to do so."

"Thanks."

"Bricks?" Esmond spoke in surprise. "Are we on to bricks again? Did you know, Antonia, that Lottie sent Mr. Ainstey a bill for bricks?"

"Yes. Paul told me. He was there just after Mr. Ainstey got the letter."

"As well as the bill," Lydia said, "there were a few hard words about trespassers and those who took what didn't belong to them."

"She's *selling* those bricks?" Dudley asked. "Those lovely bricks?"

Mrs. Merrion looked at him.

"What lovely bricks?" she asked.

"The ones that came from that tower. I saw some of them when I took Miss Purvis, sorry, Yolanda home. A fat gardener's boy was carting a wheelbarrow load across the drive. I told her they were rather special, but she didn't seem interested. She didn't even know where she could see some of them that had been used for odd bits of building down in the town."

"I don't know, either," Paul said. "Where?

"Haven't you got eyes in your head?" Dudley sounded incredulous. "That old mounting block outside the Plough. The small brick building at the back of the Church, which they were letting fall into ruin until I had a few sharp words with the Church Council."

"And the brick fireplace at the cottage," Mrs. Merrion told Esmond.

"And my stepfather's sundial," Lydia added.

"He used those bricks? Is that why he got a bill?" Dudley asked.

"He didn't get a bill for the sundial bricks. But he helped himself to a few more, and got reported by one of the gardeners. Which wasn't fair, because the sundial ones were much better than the second lot."

"What was the matter with the second lot?" Dudley asked.

"Scratches on them. Deep ones."

"Probably an inscription of some kind," Dudley said. "Builders' marks. How high was the tower when it was a tower?"

"About fourteen feet," Paul answered. "When my grandmother gave the demolition order, it must have been about six feet high. The bricks, as you know, came from the remains of the Tudor house that had stood on the site before the stone one was built."

"They didn't use many bricks in this country between Roman times and Tudor times," Dudley said. "Then there was a gradual changeover from ecclesiastical building to the domestic kind, and you find that most of the Tudor architectural masterpieces were built of brick.

Transport being what it was in those days, the bricks were local bricks, so you got a wide variety. You could put a brick into my grandfather's hands and he'd tell you, as near as makes no matter, its date and where it came from." He held out his empty glass to Paul. "Dry subject, bricks," he said.

The talk at the dinner table turned on the expedition which Paul and Lydia had made earlier in the day.

"We began with Mr. Morton at the Town Hall," Paul told them, "and went on to see the descendants of the coachman who was killed when the coach went into the river. We got nothing out of them but a small piece of newssheet which they'd come across in a drawer of a piece of furniture after the grandmother died—furniture which might have come from the Exerton house. Or might not. There was hardly anything to be seen on it, but that didn't worry Lydia; she cleared up the whole story. Tell them, Lydia."

She had to bring her mind to what he was saying; she had been studying Yolanda, and was feeling sorry for her. It was only too clear that the dress and the attempts to be friendly were directed at Dudley, all without effect. He seemed to be trying to persuade himself that she was not present. But it would take more than that, she realized, to deflate Yolanda.

"What's the story, Lydia?" Mrs. Merrion asked.

"It was just fun," Lydia said.

"Fun? It was brilliant deduction," Paul told them. "From an undecipherable word or two on that bit of paper, Lydia cleared up the whole thing. There was a man named Exerton. He was put into prison. He—"

"The word confinement was quite clear," she protested, "and there was Company with a capital C, which could have been East India Company, and there was the end of a word, -ton, which could have been Exerton."

"So Exerton was in prison," Paul went on. "His wife came to Ellstream and built their house, and that tower was built for the sole purpose of housing the loot he was going to bring with him as soon as he was released. But unfortunately he never got as far as the tower. The local interest in diving was caused by rumours that had got round about his treasure."

"Then why didn't anybody find anything?" Yolanda asked.

"There are currents in that river at that bend. Without dredging, I doubt if you could fish out pearls and diamonds from a bed of mud. And probably the diving didn't begin until the coachman's family turned up—one of his sons, if you remember, was drowned making an attempt at salvage. So there you are: everything cleared up. As a history master, Dudley, what do you think of it?"

"I wouldn't dispute it. Half the history I hammer into my pupils is unauthenticated. If this man Exerton had been in the East India Company and had been clapped into prison on his return to England, you can bet he was carrying valuables. But if so, why didn't he hand them over to his wife? I suppose there was nothing buried under the tower?"

"Nothing," Mrs. Merrion answered. "They dug deep where the tower had been, to make the foundations for the west wing of the house." She looked round the table. "Do we all go into the drawing room," she asked, "or do the men want to be left to tell funny stories?"

"We all go," Esmond said. "I'm a wanderer, and I don't get much chance to sit with charming women in drawing rooms."

While Mrs. Merrion was pouring out coffee, Yolanda put a question to Dudley.

"Has the Headmaster said anything to you about to-morrow evening?" she asked.

"No." He handed her her cup. "What's special about tomorrow evening?"

"I'm giving a show at the school, and I told him I'd have to have a master and two intelligent boys as my assistants, and I said I knew you."

"What sort of show?" Mrs. Merrion asked.

"You've all got to come and see it, but I won't tell you what it's going to be. It takes place in the school swimming bath—the indoor one. It's a thing I made up, and I do it whenever I'm near a school with a decent indoor bath. The boys pay a few pence, and the money goes to charity. Will you all promise to come? It's at half past six, and it'll only take about three quarters of an hour."

She would give no more details, but she extracted a promise from everybody to be present. Dudley pointed out that he had no choice in the matter.

It was, Mrs. Merrion thought as the guests began to leave, a successful party. There had not been much goodwill between Dudley Roach and Yolanda, but they had met and there had been no recriminations. Esmond had enjoyed his dinner. Paul, for the first time since his arrival, had looked and behaved like the old Paul, the easygoing, carefree Paul she had always known. And she had been glad of the opportunity of getting to know Lydia Cresset, who seemed to her one of the most attractive girls she had ever met.

Dudley roared away on his motorbike, creating a disturbance unusual on that quiet hillside. Paul drove Yolanda home. She paused at the door to give a message to Mrs. Merrion.

"My uncle said he'd like to come down and see you tomorrow morning. Will that be all right?"

"I'd love to see him," Mrs. Merrion said. "I hope you'll come too."

"Thank you, but I can't; I'm going to be busy. I've got

to do a rehearsal up at the school and after that I'm going over to see Sir William. I've got an idea I want to talk over with him."

"A nice girl," Esmond said when she had gone. "At least, she could be if she toned down that voice and stopped laying down the law. Lydia, you're a nice girl too; may I offer you my protection through the grounds to the border of your stepfather's property?"

"Yes. Thank you."

Paul, returning, garaged his car, found his mother had gone to bed, and decided to walk over to the cottage for a last drink with his uncle. He found him in pyjamas, stretched out on the sofa in the living room. Esmond raised a hand in greeting.

"A nice party," he said, as Paul poured out drinks and settled himself in a chair. "I wonder how your father feels when he looks down his dinner table and sees your stepmother there instead of your beautiful mother?"

"He seems contented enough."

"He was a fool to let her go. He won't feel so contented when he retires and has more leisure; your stepmother isn't a woman who'll wear well when a man has her society all day and every day. She doesn't grow on one —you found that, didn't you?"

"Yes."

"But I don't suppose he would have been happy on his own. Few men are. They say that widowers are snapped up because women feel sorry for them. My guess is that widowers are only too anxious to return to the shelter of skirts. I like that girl Lydia. Restful as well as being nice to look at. Pity she can't give some of her reposeful quality to Yolanda. Does your friend the history master know she's got her eye on him?"

"I don't know. I think he knows how to look after himself."

"If I'm any judge, she's after him. And if I'm any judge, she gets what she goes after."

"She made a bad start. And his mind isn't on women at the moment; he's got his sights on a school of his own. She wouldn't make a good Headmaster's wife—she'd be no good at making friends with the parents."

"Oh, I don't know. That heartiness might go down well—a nice, good-natured type who'd mother the boys."

"Did Lydia say much about that bill her stepfather got from Lottie?"

"He sent a cheque in payment."

"With a letter?"

"No. And no compliments. She says he's badly upset about the bill—gratuitous insult, he called it. Trust my mother to know exactly the place to stab. She's damaged his image of himself—shown him up. He'll hate her until he dies, but that won't worry her. Unless," he added reflectively, "there's a sort of stopping place on the way to heaven where they read out a list of all who've hated us, and redirect those who've got too long a list." He went on without pause. "You didn't mention your engagement, so I daresay you'd rather I didn't mention it either, but I'd like to comment, if you'll allow me to."

"Who told you about it?"

"Lydia let it out the first evening she came over and sat with me in the garden. It didn't occur to her that the members of your family wouldn't be fully informed. I used to know Mrs. Framley in my younger days. When I last saw Diana, she was about fifteen. It's no business of mine, of course—I'll save you the trouble of telling me so—but I would like to ask how they managed to manoeuvre you into the position you're in?"

In the silence that followed, Paul wondered why he felt no resentment. The feeling he had was difficult to define, but at last he identified it—it was relief. His uncle's question had driven straight to the center of his problem—and it had taken Esmond to find the right word. Manoeuvred. Manoeuvred he had undoubtedly been. Nothing could more clearly describe the events which had led to his being discarded in Ellstream, left to conjecture what was happening in Venice.

"I wish," he heard Esmond say, "that I'd been around earlier."

Paul smiled.

"What would you have done?" he asked. "Advised me to keep clear of them, as everybody else did?"

"No. That wouldn't have helped much. I've been embroiled myself, more than once, and I know, looking back, that nothing anybody said or did would have affected me much. Passion's a powerful current; if it's carrying you, having advice shouted at you from the towpath isn't much use; if you want to go, you'll keep going, and if you don't want to go and the current's too strong, you keep going anyway. All I could have done was to advise you to keep the expensive diamond ring until she came back again. You did give her an expensive diamond ring?"

"Yes."

"A pity. Has she written?"

"No."

"How are you communicating?"

"We're not."

Esmond's eyebrows went up.

"No word from her?"

"None."

"I suppose I shouldn't say this, but I've a pretty good idea who they've gone after. Have you?"

"Yes. She made no secret of it."

"Do you know him?"

"I've met him once or twice. Have you?"

"In the distant past. They won't get him."

154

"Would Mrs. Framley have made the journey unless she was sure of getting something out of it?"

"What was she risking? You were nicely trussed up, waiting for them to come back to you. How could you have been such a fool as to agree to postpone making the announcement?"

"She could hardly take her daughter on that errand if her daughter was engaged, could she?"

"Does your grandmother know anything about this?"

"I told her."

"And she said?"

"That it wouldn't come off." He paused. "She broke up your engagement, didn't she?"

"She did. You needn't fear she'll interfere with you. Her reason for interfering in my case was that if I'd married the girl I was engaged to, I would have gone to live in Canada. Lottie wouldn't have that. She wanted to keep me in England and compel me to join the Bank. Your case is quite different. And she can't touch you financially, as she could me. What are you going to do if you don't get any news from Venice? How long are you going to hang about waiting?"

"I don't know. I can't decide how long . . . how long I ought to take it. She didn't lie about her intentions. She never lied about anything—well yes, she lied about some things, but not about the things most women lie about. She told me why she was going to Venice. If I had any objections, I should have stated them then—and they would have had no effect on her."

"How did it all begin?" Esmond asked.

Paul told him. He kept back very little. He could not, he realized, have talked to anybody else with the frankness with which he spoke now to his uncle. It had needed somebody like Esmond—a man with a deep and varied knowledge of the world—a man, moreover, who knew the

Framleys and others like the Framleys, a man who above all would speak frankly but who would not attempt to influence him.

"What I didn't realize when she went to Venice," he ended, "was that I'd be left without any word from her. I suppose her idea was to wait until she could tell me something definite, one way or the other—but if so, it was a bad idea."

"Do you want her back?"

There was a long silence.

"No," Paul said at last. "I don't."

"Thank God. Let's hope she stays where she is. Did her mother ever mention my name?"

"No."

"I'm not surprised. I know too much about her. I'm regarded by my relations as some kind of amateur crook, but compared with Mrs. Framley, I'm the proverbial snowdrop. And now will you go home?" He got up and walked to the door with Paul. "Why, why, why did you have to pick on that particular girl?"

"Do I have to tell you?"

"Perhaps not. Even at fifteen, she was ... Well, good night. I'm going to walk over tomorrow morning to see Professor Errol while he's with your mother. I haven't met him for years. Who talked him into turning lecturer, for God's sake? He can't be doing it for the money—he's got enough and to spare, or he used to have. Now go away. I'm an old man and I need my sleep."

Chapter
Eight

P<small>AUL WOKE ON</small> the following morning to a room filled
with sunshine. He lay watching it lazily as it crept slowly
across the carpet, and as he did so, had the impression
that something had happened—something unusual. It
was not only that the sunshine had a different quality,
and looked as though it might last. It was not that his bed
had been placed at a different angle, or that the window
curtains were a different colour; the difference was within
himself. The unusual event was that he had slept dream-
lessly throughout the night. He had got into bed, pulled
up the covers—and slept. He had not lain awake grap-
pling with problems. He had not had a sick dawn awak-
ening to the fact that yet another day lay ahead without
word from Venice. He had slept as the tired, the satisfied,
the untroubled slept.

More. He had opened his eyes to a world in which there
appeared to be several things of interest quite unrelated
to the Framleys. Something that bound him had been

loosened. The fetters were off. And lying with the pillows punched into a ball under his head, staring at the inching bar of sunshine, he understood that at last he could think clearly. After more than a year of confusion, of mental trial and error, he found his brain clear and sharp. The world had come back into focus.

It was time, he thought, as he turned on the shower. It was high time. To have for so long lost all initiative, to have been led, tormented, raised up and cast down—passion might do that to a man—but life could not be lived for too long on a seesaw. His work had suffered, his health had suffered, his old friends had vanished and the new ones were merely part of the carnival scene in which he had acted for too long. Now at last he could draw away and study himself objectively.

He did not find the sight elevating. It was instructive, he thought as he dried himself and dressed, to discover that he could be a bigger fool than his fellow men.

His mother was having breakfast, and he saw that a place had been laid for him.

"I heard you moving upstairs, so I ordered yours with mine," she said. "There's porridge if you want it."

He lifted the lid of the dish.

"Porridge . . . I haven't had porridge for years. Any bacon and eggs?"

"Coming."

"How did you know," he asked, ladling porridge, "that I'd want a nice big breakfast this morning?"

"I didn't know. But last night, for the first time, you looked yourself. That's to say, you looked as you used to look. So I thought the air must be doing you good, and took a chance on ordering a decent breakfast for you. Will you pass the toast? And the honey, please."

"Any homemade strawberry jam?"

"I think so."

"Good. What would you say to a picnic today?"

"This isn't the picnic season. Don't put too much trust in that sun—the weather report's not optimistic. And as you ought to know by now, I'm not a picnic person. What's more, the Professor's coming to see me this morning. And this afternoon, I'm driving to meet a train that's bringing me a pair of red-crested pochards."

"Pair of what?"

"That's what it said in the catalogue. Perhaps you could buy them for my birthday."

"Aren't you getting a bit overstocked?"

"Perhaps. But they're all so beautiful. I wish I'd had them years ago. I'm sorry about the picnic. Why don't you take Lydia?"

"I will. Didn't you ever try to get on to visiting terms with the Ainsteys?"

"At first, yes. But Mr. Ainstey's antisocial, and his wife—"

"I know. Hasn't one idea beyond housekeeping." He helped himself to bacon and eggs. "She's pulling against the stream, isn't she?"

"If you believe all you read about the status of women, then yes, she is. I hope they get what they're after, whatever it is. I've always had a strong conviction that the world would have got on much better if it had been run by women. I don't want to hurt your feelings, but most men are pretty overrated. I wouldn't mind seeing that king-of-the-castle attitude knocked out of them."

"Thank you very much. I saw Esmond last night."

"Did he mention going away?"

"No. Why should he? You've made him very comfortable. Is he beginning to get on your nerves?"

"No. If it weren't for Lottie, I'd enjoy having him—but as it is, I feel they might run into one another, and the fact that they hate, really hate each other still worries me, though I ought to be used to it by now. Do you want sandwiches for this picnic you may or not be going on?"

"No, thanks. No sandwiches. I'll walk over and ask Lydia how she feels about another run in the country, with lunch thrown in."

"I like her very much."

"So do I, in a way. You never know quite whether she's with you in spirit; she gets a dreamy look at times. It's not because there's a man on her mind—it's just a difficult passage in the last quartet they rehearsed. And she's got a way of looking at you as though you'd just said something funny—but not very funny. All that's worrying her at the moment is that her stepfather might stop the allowance he makes her. It's to stop when she marries, and he's getting restive. I've an idea it isn't a large allowance, but all the same, money's money. If that fellow who runs the quartet doesn't turn up again, she'll have to find another job, and she'll need money in the interval."

"Yes, she will. About the Professor, I—"

"She's pretty badly off. She lives in a semi-basement room and shares a kitchen with hairdressers' assistants and a bathroom with God knows who. You'd think she could find another couple of girls and share a place, but that means making an effort, and I don't know whether you've noticed, but she's a girl who likes to avoid effort, unless it's playing the violin."

"Well, about this morning, can—"

"Though of course sharing a place might have its drawbacks—not for her, but for the ones who have to listen to her practising. She's nice and relaxed, but after a time you realize that what that actually means is that she sits back and lets you do all the thinking."

"There's more coffee if you—"

"It's damned unfair, when you consider it: Yolanda Purvis going round show-jumping, mostly on other people's horses, and visiting people like Lottie and driving her uncle round the—"

"She doesn't drive him. He's terrified in cars unless they're driven by highly trained chauffeurs."

"Well, she accompanies him. While Lydia Cresset is stuck underground with half a kitchen and a tenth of a bathroom."

"Yes. Is it definite that you'll be out to lunch?"

"Not that she makes— What did you say?"

"I asked if you'd be out to lunch."

"Yes."

"Lydia might not want to have lunch out."

"On the other hand, she might. Do we really have to go to this show of Yolanda's this evening?"

"Yes. We'll go in my car, and take Lydia and Esmond—and Lydia's aunt too, if she'd care to come. Will you ask her?"

"If I remember."

He went to Mr. Ainstey's the long way round. Brenda opened the door.

"Good morning. If you want Mr. Ainstey," she said, "he's gone for a long walk. You'll find him up in the woods, brooding on whether he'll use those bricks or throw them at your grandmother. If you want me, I'm busy. If you want Lydia, she's gone over to the cottage to see your uncle. You may find yourself in the way; she discovered last night that he once played the cello in the school orchestra, and they're going on from there. May I go back to work?"

"Yes. Would you care to go with us this evening at six-thirty to a show of some mysterious kind that—"

"Oh, Lydia said there was to be something of the kind. No, I don't think so, thank you."

He crossed the lawn to the cottage. Outside it were two comfortable chairs; on them were Lydia and his uncle. He joined them and was given a somewhat abstracted greeting.

"No, Lydia," his uncle continued. "You've got the date wrong. *Fidelio* was first produced in Vienna in 1805. Get yourself a chair, Paul. And drinks for three."

"Drinks? You said you were going over to the house to see the Professor."

"All in good time, all in good time. It's the 1814 revised version with a new overture that you're thinking of, Lydia. The three Leonora overtures were called one, two and three, but they were composed in 1807, 1805 and 1806 respectively. You see how confusing? Did you know that Henry the Fifth composed?"

"No."

"He did. So did Henry the Eighth."

"So did I, once," Lydia said. "I wrote a new setting for the school hymn, but I jazzed it up a bit, so they stuck to the traditional air. When's the last time you played the cello?"

Esmond closed his eyes and counted. Opening them again, he said that the answer came to forty.

"You'll be out of practice," Paul remarked. "What'll you drink, Lydia—this or this?"

"Neither, thank you. It's too early."

"I went to your house to see if you felt like a drive."

"Me too?" Esmond asked.

"No, not you too," Paul answered. "You're going to see the Professor."

But there was no need to go. Coming across from Mrs. Merrion's house were Mrs. Merrion and Professor Errol. They paused to study the waterfowl, and Esmond rose and went to join them.

"I thought it would be nice to have lunch out," Paul said to Lydia. "There are only two directions you can go in or around Ellstream—you can go along the valley that way, or along the valley *that* way. Coming?"

"Sounds nice. Thank you."

The Professor, joining them, said that Yolanda had given him a lift as far as the gate.

"Lady Charlotte lent her the car to go to Sir William's," he explained. "She's got a scheme she wants to talk over with him." He sighed. "An energetic young woman. Yes, very. Like her mother." He chose the most comfortable chair and settled himself in it. "So here I am all by myself. Don't think for a moment that I don't appreciate all the interest Yolanda and her mother take in me. But for them, I should sit and do nothing whatsoever. And of course I should give up lecturing."

"Would you mind that so much?" Mrs. Merrion asked.

"To be honest, no." He peered at the amount of liquid Esmond was pouring into his glass. "Oh thank you, thank you, that's enough. What was I saying? Ah yes, lecturing. I should like very much to give it up. There is nothing I should like more than to give it up." He leaned forward and dropped his voice to a whisper. "As a matter of fact, I'm not at all good at it. But my sister," he went on in his normal tones, "and Yolanda herself persuaded me to make the effort." He raised his glass, bowed and drank. "So I suppose that I must go on with it, and I daresay it's better than allowing myself to vegetate."

His voice—slow, high, musical—added to the restful quality of the day. It was more like July than May—a day with an extra spice of enjoyment because weather like this, at this season, could not possibly last.

The little stone-built house to which Paul took Lydia for lunch was one with a modest sign marking it a restaurant. It was built at the juncture of two roads, in a position so exposed that Paul told her of the occasions on which he had had to run from car to restaurant to escape the bitter winds. But today was windless, and they went in and were shown to a table on which the sun was making the knives flash.

"This was a cowman's house once," he told her. "Then he won the triple on the pools, so what did he do?"

"Turned it into a restaurant."

"Don't go so fast. I was about to list all the things he could have done with all that money."

"And didn't do?"

"He divided it into eight equal parts, dished out seven parts to his mother, father and five brothers—and used the eighth share to install his wife in this restaurant. She was a cook before she married him, and wasn't getting enough scope. Now she's happy because they have customers, but not too many customers. She'll give us roast beef, Yorkshire pudding, potatoes that have been roasted round the joint, rather overdone cabbage, and after that, apple tart with cheese. I won't ask if you're hungry, because I've noticed that you like to eat. You must be very expensive to feed."

"Not when I'm feeding myself." She finished her roll of bread, reached over to take his, buttered it and took a bite. "I told you—the can opener."

"You must cook yourself a decent meal sometimes," he said.

Her eyes, mildly speculative, rested on him.

"Did you ever make any attempt to find out how the other half lives?" she asked.

"I didn't do any extensive research, no."

"I'd like to do some now, if you don't object. You live in your own rooms?"

"Apartment."

"You have a man to look after you?"

"I have."

"Of course. Who'd polish your shoes? You have a chauffeur?"

"I borrow my father's if I need one."

"So how can you picture people who have to live on

164

lower levels? Could you get some more of this heavenly bread from that other table?"

He got it.

"Anything else?"

"More butter, if you can order some. Please."

He ordered it.

"I'll miss your uncle," she said.

His eyebrows went up.

"Who's leaving—he or you?"

"He says he may be going in a day or two. He says something's come up. Something good, he hopes. I hope so too."

"We all hope so. But it's a recurrent theme: he comes, he hears of something good, he goes. If you wait long enough, he'll be back. I'm glad you like him."

"Perhaps I feel safe because I've got nothing he wants. If I had, I suppose he'd help himself to it?"

"Without any doubt."

"I don't understand. He belongs to a rich family. He must have something to live on."

"He had. You don't understand because you regard him as a man who'd act dishonestly only if he was driven to it. I suppose you could say that Lottie drove him to it, but that wouldn't be true; he could have cut himself off from her without going to the lengths he did. But his aim was to hurt, and you can do the most damage if you attack your enemy on his weak side. Lottie's weakness is her inordinate pride—and that's what Esmond went for. Lottie's an anachronism. I live the way I do because I can afford it—but I regard my way of life as overprivileged and to a certain extent, out of date. I'm grateful for the things I have, more grateful because I don't know how long I'll have them. But Lottie's convinced that she and her family are something special; her sons were reared on the lesson that they must be upright and brave and true and so on and so on because they were who they were. She had a very personal interpretation of *noblesse oblige;* she narrowed it down to fit. So when her elder son realized how much he loathed her, he merely shed all the virtues she regarded as peculiarly Merrion ones. He only kept within the law because he said prison would be uncomfortable. Nobody has ever been able to pin anything on him, but he has done, and he has seen to it that his mother knows he has done, some dirty deeds. And hard as she is, he knows that it hurts. It's the only way he could get his own back for what he calls the years of hell she put him through. Have I made him clearer?"

"I suppose so. So he'll go away and you won't know where he is?"

"No. This is an even smaller world than it used to be; you'd think someone would meet him somewhere at some time—but nobody ever has. We don't know whether he vanishes to the same place each time, or chooses a new one. We don't know what he does. I'd like to think he had a woman, perhaps children too, somewhere, but somehow I get the feeling that he hasn't; he's on his own. One thing I think my sister and I owe him: Lottie never attempted to interfere with anything we did. Apart from lining up girls for me to marry, and men for my sister to fall in love with, she left us alone. When Esmond went, she seemed to retire from combat. We got, and get from her, frequent blasts —she's got a hellish temper—but that's as far as she goes."

"I wish I'd known my grandparents. They died before I was born."

"Do your sisters look like you?"

"No. They're dark, like my father. It's not much fun to come right at the tail of a family; I was just beginning to catch up and have fun with my sisters when they left home."

"They all got married?"

"My mother thinks so, but only two of them did. The third one's living with a Canadian who's got a lunatic father who made him promise he wouldn't marry until he was thirty. That'll be next year. When my mother goes to stay with them, it's all right, because she thinks they're married, but when his father comes over on a visit, it's not so easy."

"Does your aunt know?"

"No. She wouldn't mind, but I've never told her. She hates men."

"What did men do to her?"

"Nothing. She got married once, for a whole week. All she'll tell you about why she left is that she thought it all a great waste of time. If you press her, she adds that after a hard day's work, she likes to get her sleep. I met her ex once—he dropped in to a concert and came round to look at me afterwards because he saw my name on the programme and remembered it."

"Had he remarried?"

"No. He said a week was more than enough."

He studied her in silence for a time.

"Ever been in love?" he asked.

"Part of the way. I've thought: This is it. But it wasn't. I'd wake up one morning, and the feeling had gone. I wish I could meet a man who has the effect on me that some music has. Haydn. Naturally, being a string quartet, we cover quite a lot of Haydn, and sometimes I find myself trembling—I don't mean shaking like ague, I mean inside. At times, it's . . . You're not listening."

"I'm listening, and wondering. How can a girl be such a mixture of the spiritual and the earthy? Trembling over Haydn and eating like a horse. I'd like to find out how many other musicians grow pale with ecstasy thinking of Haydn, while getting through roast beef and Yorkshire pudding and potatoes. I suppose one feeds the other?"

She was looking at him in surprise.

"You're different today," she said. "At least, you seem different."

"I feel different. Have you any idea what Yolanda's going to do in the school bath this evening?"

"No."

"I suppose you wouldn't care to dine with me afterwards and put on your long brocade dress and a tiara? There's a card on my mother's desk inviting her and her family to something called the Ellstream May Festival. Entrance one pound per person, proceeds to charity, dance music by the Ellstream Amateur Eight. Interested?"

"You mean make up a party and—"

"No. No party. Yourself, myself. Then if we don't like it, we can slip away without emptying the hall. Will you come?"

"I forgot my tiara."

"Careless. I suggested dinner first because although they're providing supper, all you'll get will be chicken and ham sandwiches and meat pies and trifle and treacle tart and fruit cake and walnut cake and chocolate cake. Can you survive on that?"

"Yes. Thank you."

Nobody who was present that evening at the school indoor swimming bath ever forgot the occasion. Perhaps the element of surprise contributed something to the success of the show. The Headmaster announced simply that it was called "Lights on Water," and added that it would consist of two unrelated scenes, with a ten-minute interval between them. The boys, filing in and taking their places, felt no anticipatory pleasure; prep had been suspended in order that they might attend, but they would rather have been shown a film than a performance by an unknown Miss Purvis.

At six-thirty precisely, Yolanda appeared from a dressing room. She was wearing a black frogman suit which left only her face visible, and she carried what looked to be long pieces of wood with lights fixed on them. There were three assistants: Dudley Roach and two senior boys, and their first act was to switch off all the lights, plunging the place into total darkness. Not a gleam of illumination was allowed to enter; paper had been pasted along any crevice that might admit light. Then two small pinpoints of light appeared—the miniature torches of the boys, who were in charge of the musical arrangements. On their knees could be discerned record players. Between the boys stood Dudley Roach with a supply of cassettes.

Total darkness, total silence. There was the sound of a subdued splash, and the next moment Yolanda made a brief announcement.

"The first part of the programme," she said, "is called Highway Robbery."

That was all. But on the water appeared lights, and at the same moment came the sound of horses' hooves—a steady beat that accompanied the progress of what every spectator realized was a coach. On it went, with an occasional crack of the driver's whip, and the sound of voices and laughter. More lights in the distance, coming nearer: two horsemen, who reined in their horses to greet their friends in the coach. All eyes were on the steadily moving lights on the water; every boy in the audience had begun to visualize the scene, had begun to follow the progress of the coach along the highway, round curves, through stretches of shallow water. The two horsemen rode on; then one wheeled, returned and asked whether the coach driver had heard of the presence of highwaymen in the dreaded woods ahead? Yes, the coachman knew, but he and the postillion were armed, as were the two gentlemen travelling in the coach. Then all was well, said the horse-man, and galloped away to join his companion.

A slight increase of tension; was there, a lady passenger asked timidly, any danger? What danger? her husband wanted to know. She had the protection of himself and three other armed men; what could she fear? Soon they would be in London; they had but fifteen miles to go. They were to stop for a change of horses; if there was any news of highwaymen, they would get it at the Inn.

There were bright lights at the Inn, and a bustle of arrival and departure. The lady was assisted to alight; the windows of the Inn could be seen, and the interior imag-ined, warm and comfortable—and safe. While the trav-ellers refreshed themselves, the coachman joined other drivers; over their ale, they dismissed the dangers of the road. If travellers armed themselves, there was nothing to fear.

On once more. The bright, busy Inn fell behind; ahead was the dark, the increasingly lonely road. A silence—the silence of apprehension—fell for a moment on the trav-ellers and on the audience. For a time nothing was heard but the clip-clop of hooves, the crack of the whip—so that the sudden tumult of the challenge, the shouts, the shrieks—and the shots—burst on the school unawares and made every boy's heart thump. A holdup. Along the ranks of boys, a low murmur broke out; it mounted and became a roar. The roar augmented the sounds of the running battle being enacted on what every spectator now firmly believed to be a wooded section of the high-way outside London. Shots, more shots, more shrieks. The scream of a horse. The surrender of the coachman and his passengers—and then a sudden clatter of hooves from the direction of London. Soldiers! Soldiers to the rescue! Sol-diers surrounding the coach, soldiers rounding up the highwaymen, soldiers chasing those who attempted to get away.

It was almost impossible, during this climax, to hear the sounds coming from the cassettes; the audience had taken up the story and was following it to the end. The capture, the gradual dying away of the sounds of battle, the restored calm of the travellers and the final lineup of the cavalcade to finish the journey under strong escort—throughout, every boy in the audience became an actor, part of the action, exhausted as the sounds of hooves died away in the distance.

The lights went on. The spectators, confused, blinking, sat for a moment disentangling fact from fiction. Then Yolanda was seen climbing out of the water—and there was a roar of applause. Dudley Roach held her towelling robe; she put it on, raised her hand in acknowledgement and returned to her dressing room.

The second half might have proved an anticlimax—but it was, if possible, a greater success than the first half had been. Dudley Roach announced that Miss Purvis would recreate for them the Battle of Trafalgar. In case there were boys present who had forgotten the facts they had been taught, let him now remind them that the battle was fought on the 21st of October, 1805, between the British, and the combined French and Spanish fleets off Cape Trafalgar, about thirty miles northwest of the Strait of Gilbraltar. The British fleet, commanded by Nelson, consisted of twenty-seven ships of the line, mounting 2.138 guns. The Franco-Spanish force, commanded by Villeneuve, consisted of thirty-three sail, with 2.640 guns. No British ships were lost in the battle. Fifteen enemy ships were taken or destroyed. Nelson was mortally wounded during the battle—but he had lived to command one of the world's decisive naval victories, and he had foiled Napoleon's threat to invade England.

Audience participation was greater throughout the battle than it had been during the previous half of the programme. When news came of Nelson's mortal wound, the silence of death fell on the spectators. A dim glow illumined the scene of his passing—and then the uproar of battle was heard again, and the cries of triumph and the confusion of ships moving out of the line of fire. When the lights went up, the boys rose to their feet and cheered. Yolanda drew her assistants forward to receive their share of the applause. The Headmaster came down to shake her hand and to make a brief speech of thanks.

Dudley was feeling a little confused. The originality of the performance had roused his admiration, but he could not think of a way of offering congratulations that would sound sincere without sounding too friendly. He was not a man who had ever had any exaggerated idea of his own charms, but it had become obvious to him that this girl moved fast, and was moving in his direction. He had known many women in his life who had met him halfway; this was the first one who had advanced at her own pace and, in the most determined manner, was backing him into a corner.

He carried the last of the props to the dressing room. When he returned, Yolanda was addressing the two boys.

"You were wonderful," she said. "Not a hitch. You synchronized the sound marvellously, and what's more, you kept clear of the electric cables. Jolly good."

"You going to do any more shows, Miss Purvis?" they wanted to know.

"One day, perhaps. Now run along, or you'll be late for the special supper the Headmaster's putting on. Thank you both very much indeed."

They went away, but the exchange had given Dudley time to decide on the form his congratulations would take. He would be not warm, but wary. He would give her her due, and then he would escape before she could trap him into escorting her to the dining room, where she was to be the guest of honour.

"I'd like to say," he began, "that the show went—"

He got no further. Yolanda's hand came down with a heavy thump on his shoulder.

"Dudley, you were simply mag-*nificent*. I can't tell you how wonderful it was to be able to do my part of it and know that you were there, giving the boys their cue right on time, never putting a foot wrong."

"Oh, that's all right. I wanted to say—"

"I shall never give a performance in this school again unless you're my assistant. I shall tell the Headmaster so."

"Don't bother. I—"

"It's no bother, I assure you. Whenever I can put in a word for my friends, I like to do it. A word in the right ear, if you follow me. I've got Sir William in my pocket, you know. Eating out of my hand, so if there's anything I can do for you in that direction, you've only to ask."

"Well, I—"

"Everybody knows that you're a first-class master, but everybody can do with a little push, don't you agree?"

"No." Another sentence like that, he thought furiously, spoken in that tone of patronage, and he'd push her back into the water. "No, I don't agree. Is there anything else you'd like put away? If not, you'd better get dressed and hurry along to the dining room."

"Wait while I change, will you? I've asked the Headmaster to put you next to me. We can go along together."

The dressing room door closed behind her. He walked to the edge of the water and stared into its green depths, seeking help.

Chapter
Nine

PAUL, WAKING LATE on the following morning, went downstairs to a solitary breakfast. He was about to begin when his mother addressed him through the window that opened onto the garden.

"Good morning. Two messages for you," she said. "The first from Lottie—she wants to see you, and soon."

"Trouble?"

"I don't know. It was Joseph who rang. The other message was from Dudley Roach, who says he'll be having cold beef and pickles in the Plough at one o'clock and would be glad if you'd join him. Did you and Lydia enjoy the May Carnival?"

"Yes and no. That hall was built to hold a hundred, and they crammed in three times that number. And they kept holding up the proceedings to raffle things."

"I hope they made a lot of money. Esmond looked in on his way to town, to see if I wanted anything. Shut this window, will you? There's a breeze coming up."

He finished his breakfast and walked up to his grandmother's house. A summons from her almost invariably meant that she had blown a small incident up to disproportionate size—but when Joseph opened the door and led him in the direction of the drawing room, he realized that this was a serious matter; only when she was at her most angry did she hold interviews in the drawing room.

She was standing in the middle of the room, and for once, spoke without preliminaries.

"Good morning. I will not ask you to sit down. I'm extremely angry. I have something to show you. Will you come with me, please?"

Throwing a shawl over her shoulders, she turned towards the long window that opened onto a terrace. He opened it, and followed her out. She said nothing until they had crossed the lawn and were going in the direction of the kitchen garden; then she spoke in the abrupt tone she used when upset.

"Bricks," she said. "You know, I suppose, that that man Ainstey came into my grounds and helped himself to as many as he wanted?"

"Yes. You sent him a bill."

"He paid it. But I took the precaution of having the bricks moved from the far end of the grounds to a corner of the kitchen garden. They were placed in piles, stacked in an orderly manner, not thrown down anyhow, as they were before. I came out yesterday to inspect the work. Nothing could have been neater. You will now see what happened to them during the night."

She had paused before the high wooden door that gave entrance to the walled enclosure. They went in, skirted rows of neatly aligned vegetables, walked along paths close to a south wall on which peach branches were outspread, and then reached a far corner of the garden. His grandmother stopped, and with a gesture, indicated what she had brought him here to see.

He found himself looking at a scattered pile of bricks. A few still remained on top of one another, but the rest were thrown over a wide area. His grandmother spoke in a voice husky with rage.

"Your friend, Mr. Ainstey," she said. "A cheap revenge. I may call him your friend, may I not, since you have become so intimate with his stepdaughter? He paid the bill I sent him and then made up his mind to—"

"No. I don't believe it." Paul spoke with conviction. "I don't know who did a stupid and useless thing like this, but I'm certain it wasn't Mr. Ainstey."

"And I'm certain it was. About a dozen bricks are missing. That proves—"

"It doesn't prove anything. Why would he want to come here in the night and mess about with piles of bricks?"

"I've told you. He can't hurt me, he can only do his best to annoy me. The bricks themselves are not what I'm angry about; it's the fact that he has for the third time trespassed on my property. He's gone too far. I'm going to report the matter to the police."

Paul stared at her.

"You can't be serious?"

"I am perfectly serious."

"You can't take a . . . a trifling little affair like this to the police," he protested. "You'd be wasting your time —and theirs. No damage has been done; somebody's walked off with a few bricks, that's all. There's not the smallest proof that Mr. Ainstey had anything to do with it."

"That is what I want you to find out. That is why I sent for you. I want you to tell him that I have reason to believe that this is his work, but before going to the police, I shall give him a chance of clearing himself."

"Why go to those lengths? Why not take it, if you want to, as an attempt on his part to work off his spleen—and then forget it?"

"I don't think you've given the matter enough thought," she said coldly. "I am an elderly woman living alone. I have servants, but no dogs to guard the house. There are efficient burglar alarms, but I should like to be reassured that my grounds are not full of prowlers every night. I shall explain this to the police. They will question Mr. Ainstey, and if there is no proof that he is involved, the matter will go no further. But with the police in his house, it will have gone far enough. He won't forget it."

They walked back to the house.

"You want me to talk to him first?" he asked.

"Yes. Make it clear to him that it's my firm intention to take the matter to the police."

He went home and reported the meeting to his mother, and she spoke in a tone that held no doubt.

"She will, of course," she said. "And she'll do it for the reason she gave: to humiliate him. Are you quite sure he had nothing to do with it?"

"Of course. Aren't you?"

"Yes. That's to say, I can't imagine him doing anything so idiotic. All the same, he's a hot-tempered man, and he must be feeling sore about that bill she sent him. People in rages do foolish things."

"I daresay. But he's got his share of pride, and I can't see him descending to schoolboy level like this. I suppose I'll have to go and see him?"

"Yes. It's better for him to hear about it from you."

"Why does she always create these situations? Isn't this a case for remembering that proverb about the dogs barking but the caravan passing on?"

"She has never passed on. In my knowledge of her, she has always stopped and dealt with the dogs. If you're going, I advise you to go now and get it done with. You won't find Lydia at the house; she went down to the town with Esmond."

He decided to take the shortcut. The doors and windows of the cottage were closed. Through the bordering shrubs, he saw to his annoyance that Mr. Ainstey was working on the base of the sundial. He would rather have found him anywhere else. To speak of bricks, and thefts, and trespass while standing by the evidence, was not going to make matters easier.

Mr. Ainstey, he found, was in a mood almost as sour as his grandmother's. His greeting was a grunt.

"I'd rather you didn't come that way," he said. "Your grandmother talks too much about trespass, but you're certainly giving a good imitation. There's a front door, and the bell works."

"I'm sorry. I—"

"It's Lydia's fault for skipping backwards and forwards to get to that damned cottage. She's not in. She went down to town with your uncle."

"I know. It was you I came to see. It's not a pleasant errand, but I'm under orders from my grandmother."

Mr. Ainstey, who had picked up a spade, put it down again.

"Oh? Another bill?" he asked. "Let's have it."

"The bricks which used to be up at the back of her grounds were moved to a corner of the kitchen garden. They were piled neatly, and for some reason, counted. Last night, somebody went in, messed up all the piles and left the bricks lying around. About a dozen of them are missing."

Mr. Ainstey stared at him with a frown.

"What's all that got to do with me?" he demanded.

179

"Why don't you get to the point, if there is a point?"

"The point is that my grandmother thinks you might have had something to do with it, and I can't convince her that—"

He stopped. Mr. Ainstey's face had turned a deep shade of purple.

"She . . . she s-suggests that . . . that . . ." The savage stuttering was checked by a visible effort. "You mean to stand there and tell me calmly that that wicked old . . . that next-to-witch, that harridan, has gone as far as to . . . Is she off her head? Does she imagine she can treat people like this? You ought to be ashamed of yourself for coming here with a story like that. You're a man, aren't you? Or are you? Do you let her use you to carry her insults round? You can go back and tell her that if she has any suspicion I went into her kitchen garden and stole bricks, she can call in the police and let them handle the matter."

"That's why I came. She's going to report it."

"To the police?"

"Yes."

"Giving my name as suspect number one?"

"I'm afraid so. I told her I was certain you had nothing whatsoever to do with it, but—"

"You think that would stop her from dragging me in? What does she want from me—a denial? A confession? What makes you think she'd take my word for anything? I've told you what she is—a wicked old harridan. I did my best to keep clear of her for years. God knows why I was such a twice-damned fool as to take that second lot of bricks. I don't believe for one moment that she thinks I entered her grounds last night—but it's a splendid opportunity to make herself unpleasant and spread venom, and she's going to make the most of it. You can tell her to call in the local police and a squad from Scotland Yard too, if she wants to. And now you can go away. If you come back, which I hope you won't, come round to the front. Then we can let you in—or not, as we please. Good morning to you."

He picked up the spade and leaned on it watching Paul go back the way he had come. His fury had made him tremble; as it drained out of him, he found himself left with a feeling he had never in his life experienced. He took some time to identify it, and at last realized with amazement and incredulity that what he was feeling was a vast loneliness. He wanted his wife. He wanted her so badly that he felt himself shaking again, and decided to go indoors. He longed to talk to somebody, and the person he had in mind was his wife. She would listen without arguing; his great need at this moment was not comfort, but to be comforted. But he was alone, and she would not be back for another two weeks, and who could tell what further humiliation that wicked old woman next door would not subject him to before her return? Two weeks . . .

It had begun to rain when Paul drove down to meet Dudley Roach at the Plough. He left his car in the car park nearby and went on a swift tour of the shops to see if he could find Lydia in any of them. She was nowhere to be seen; his uncle had also vanished. It was with a feeling of irritation that he at last entered the Plough, and it mounted when he saw Lydia and his uncle comfortably seated near a fire which Dudley was sharing. They greeted him with upraised glasses.

"You're late," Dudley told him. "You shouldn't keep a fellow waiting in a pub—it makes him order refills."

"Lydia and I ran into Dudley," Esmond explained, "and he took us round the town showing us all those pockets of bricks he'd located. Sit down. Lydia and I are joining this beef-and-pickle party. Dudley's paying for you. You—I trust—will pay for Lydia and for me. Is that all right?"

Paul said, not graciously, that he supposed it was, and ordered another round of drinks. Dudley studied him.

"Something the matter?" he asked.

"Yes. My grandmother. She moved those blasted bricks to the kitchen garden and somebody got in last night and played havoc with the neat piles they'd been put into—and walked off with a dozen or so."

"She *counted* the bricks?" Esmond asked in astonishment.

"She must have done—or somebody must have done it for her." Paul answered. "But that's not what's worrying me; it's her threat—and as you know, she always carries out that kind of threat—to call in the police."

"What—for a dozen missing bricks?" Dudley asked. "Who, incidentally, would want a dozen bricks?"

"She said Mr. Ainstey took them, out of what she called cheap revenge."

"She thinks he went prowling and stole bricks?" Lydia asked in a tone of stupefaction. "That's absurd."

"So I told her."

"She'd better not let him know she thinks that," she warned. "He's apt to get violent when roused."

"She sent me to talk to him."

"You went?" Esmond asked.

"I went. It was better for him to hear it from me, wasn't it, than to open the door to a posse of policemen?"

"There's no problem about getting into the grounds," Dudley commented. "That's a fine, imposing gateway, but I bet I could make an entry anywhere round the perimeter. Why didn't she accuse me of swiping the bricks? I'm the one who told her they were unusual."

"Perhaps after this," Esmond said, "she'll agree to keep a dog. Did she actually see the neat piles, or did she take the gardener's word for it?"

"She went out and inspected them," Paul answered. "And while Mr. Ainstey isn't my favourite type of step-father, I can't see him involved in a thing like this."

"He's no night prowler," Lydia said. "He likes his sleep. This is going to spoil all the fun he was having, making the base for his sundial. Perhaps I ought to go home and see if I can do anything."

"All in good time," Esmond said. "We're going to eat first. I'll have my beef in sandwich form, I think. And tell them to put on plenty of mustard, will you, Paul?"

Dudley got up to help with the carrying of the food. They pushed two tables together and began to eat. Dudley bit into a thick sandwich and spoke in an aggrieved voice.

"Nobody's asked me if I've got any troubles," he complained. "Why should I have come all this way down to pay for food when I could have eaten up at the school for nothing?"

"Tell us," Esmond invited.

"I came here to talk to Paul, to find out if he'd heard the news."

"What news?" Paul asked.

Dudley shifted in his chair and faced him.

"Have you heard any rumours going round about a riding school?" he asked.

"No. The one in town packed up a long time ago, and as far as I know, there's never been any talk of starting another."

"That was before Yolanda Purvis got here. This morning I was told on the best authority—the Headmaster's—that she's been petitioning the school Governors to let her open a riding school for the boys."

There was a pause.

"Does the Headmaster want a riding school?" Paul asked.

"He could do without one. But if the Board of Governors tell him he's got to have one, he'll have one, won't he? And that's not all. The riding school, if opened, which it will be, is to be at the school. There's a plan to fix up the old Dutch barn as an indoor school, and the fields beyond the outdoor swimming pool will be a kind of circus ring with jumps or hoops or whatever it is the pupils have to go through or over."

"Do the boys want a riding school?" Lydia asked.

"The boys? The boys'll welcome anything that takes them out of class."

"What's your worry?" Paul asked. "You won't have anything to do with it, will you?"

"You think not?" Dudley spoke bitterly. "Did you see me at her water sports, assistant in chief? She picked me. The Headmaster says she's picked me to act as liaison officer between the school and the riding school. Can you picture my future? There'll be no place to hide. I'll be under orders from Yolanda Purvis, being bossed around. Human dynamo, she is. How long has she been here? A couple of days—and look: books in the mud, a visit to the school to offer me dough, water sports—and a riding school. She hasn't really got started yet."

"She can start a riding school without worrying you too much, can't she?" Lydia asked.

"She could, but she won't. She scares me. You can brush off the average girl if you really try, but this one seems to have a kind of built-in resistance to . . . to resistance. You can state objections, but you might just as well address them to the wall. So I asked Paul to come down and tell me if he can think of anything anyone can do to scotch this riding school scheme."

"I suppose she got at the Governors through Sir William?" Paul asked.

"He's in her pocket. Her own words."

Silence fell. Nobody had any reassurance to offer. At

last, Dudley gathered up his mackintosh, paid his share of the bill and departed.

"She'll get her riding school," Esmond commented. "And if she wants Dudley, she'll get him too."

"Would it be such a bad thing if he did?" Lydia asked. "He wants a school; she wants a riding school. She's bossy, but then, so is he in a way. They might make a good pair."

She stood up. Esmond refused Paul's offer of a lift.

"No, thanks. Take Lydia back. I've got things to do. Thanks for the beef and so on—I enjoyed myself."

He left them. Paul looked at Lydia.

"Ready?"

"Yes." As they walked to the car, she spoke in an anxious tone.

"I'm worried about my stepfather."

"Don't be. There's nothing you can do about it."

There was no need for anybody to do anything about it. On the following morning, Mr. Ainstey went into his garden to find his sundial a confused heap of bricks on the lawn. He bent, stricken, to gather them into some kind of order—and discovered that several were missing.

Chapter
Ten

NOT EVEN LADY CHARLOTTE could make herself believe that Mr. Ainstey had destroyed his own sundial; the blame for the disappearance of a dozen bricks from her kitchen garden must therefore be placed elsewhere. As for Mr. Ainstey, he was stunned; nothing in his life had given him the pleasure and satisfaction that the building of the sundial—his first essay in manual labour—had done. Now his work was in ruins.

Esmond, seeing him standing on the lawn, gazing at the destruction, came, unrebuked, to stand beside him and offer sympathy.

"Wanton." Mr. Ainstey cleared the hoarseness from his throat. "Wanton. The work of devils."

"You heard nothing during the night?"

"Nothing. And it isn't as though I'm a heavy sleeper. If there'd been a sound, I would have heard it."

"It could hardly," Esmond suggested gently, "have been done without noise of some kind."

"If they got an iron bar as a wedge, they could have gone about it a bit at a time. The lawn would have muffled the sound of the bricks falling."

"Perhaps. If you'd like help in putting it up again, I'd be—"

"Eight missing."

"Eight bricks—missing?"

"Yes."

"Are you quite sure?"

"Absolutely certain. Why in God's name would anyone want to cart away eight bricks? Eight from here, a dozen from your mother's lot. Lunacy. That's what it is: lunacy. There's some chap running round loose who ought to be under a psychiatrist's care. What I'd like to get hold of is not the police—what the devil could they do?—but a few doctors, to ask whether any of their patients have lost their wits in the past week or so."

"Lydia and your sister-in-law heard nothing?"

"Nothing. One of them—my sister-in-law—thought she saw a light."

"A torch?"

"Probably. This couldn't have been done in total darkness. There was a moon, but it wouldn't have given enough light for this job."

Esmond turned to Lydia, who had come out of the house to join them.

"Bad business," he said.

"She was the first to see it," Mr. Ainstey said.

Remembering the look he had seen on her face as they had surveyed the damage together, a look of sick disgust and anger, Mr. Ainstey felt that in certain circumstances, he might bring himself to like her.

"What's so awful," she said after a time, "is that it's so . . . so reasonless. You could understand someone stealing money or watches or ornaments. In a garden, you could understand them digging up a rare plant and going off with it—but *bricks?*"

"I've got to go down to the town," Esmond told Mr. Ainstey. "Can I do anything for you while I'm there?"

"No, thanks. Good of you, but I'll be going down myself later on."

"How about you, Lydia?"

"I'll stay here. I rang up Paul and he's coming to look at this mess."

"Then I won't see you until this evening. I've got a lot to do, and I'll drop into the Plough for another cold lunch."

He went back to the cottage. Mr. Ainstey went indoors, but Lydia was still standing by the sundial when Paul appeared, using the garden approach in what he felt to be special circumstances. His reaction to the sight of the damage was almost as strong as Esmond's had been, but he had no suggestions to make about the possible culprits.

"We'll all help him to put it up again," he said. "I've told my grandmother, and she agrees that your stepfather would hardly have kicked his sundial to pieces to remove suspicion from himself. Are you coming down to town?"

"No. I want to go somewhere quiet. I want to think."

"So do I. What are Esmond's plans?"

"He's going down and staying down to lunch." She turned towards the house. "If you'll wait a few minutes, I'll be ready to go."

They met Mrs. Merrion near the waterfowl enclosure.

"I saw what happened to the sundial," she told Lydia. "When I heard what had happened, I went up to the boundary and looked across. I'm so sorry for your stepfather."

She joined them as they walked to the garage for Paul's car. As they went, she spoke in a puzzled tone.

"Did either of you run into the Professor yesterday?"

"No. Why?" Paul asked.

"He's on his way over to see me. He says he's got news. He wouldn't tell me what it was."

"Then I will," Paul said. "It'll have something to do with a riding school."

"But that's nothing to do with him, is it?"

"His niece. Dudley Roach says there's going to be a riding school at St. Godfric's. Run by Yolanda."

Mrs. Merrion spoke thoughtfully.

"It wouldn't be a bad thing for the school," she said, "and she'd be a good person to run it. Let's see what the Professor has to say about it."

The Professor was unable to say very much, for when he arrived, Yolanda was with him. They had walked across from Lady Charlotte's house, and the Professor was looking pink after the pace she had set.

"News!" she called, as soon as they were within earshot. "Three guesses. I've just told Lady Charlotte, and she said it was a sensible idea—coming from her, that's high praise. And of course, Sir William knows all about it, and so do the members of the Board he managed to get hold of. Can you guess what I'm going to do?"

"Open a riding school," Paul said.

"Oh, how *mean* of you to guess straightaway! Yes, that's what it is. When I heard that there were over two hundred boys in the school, and not a single horse, I made up my mind and went to see Sir William and talked to him. He was absolutely marvellous; he didn't raise a single objection, but he said that of course he couldn't help me until he'd been in touch with the other Governors. He was on my side from the start. It isn't as though I'm putting the school to any expense; all I need is permission to establish my riding school in the school grounds. I'll pay all the expenses, and of course I'll take a proportion of the fees to give myself a profit. There's magnificent riding country behind the school—Sir William and I drove up to look at it. He spent hours on the phone getting in touch with the other Governors to get their reactions, and he said that as far as he could see, there isn't an objection in sight." She paused. "There's only one tiny flaw: my uncle."

Everybody looked at the tiny flaw, to find it beaming.

"It's really a splendid idea, splendid. She's been wanting to do it for years. Years. What she means about the flaw is that—"

"He's being sweet about it," Yolanda broke in, "but it means I can't go on this lecture tour with him. There's too much to be done here. As I said to Sir William, one has to strike while the iron's hot, and if I leave now, things'll sag. So we're going to call off the lectures."

"I'll give it up," the Professor said. "Never was any good at it. Not up on a platform, anyway. Might do a bit on television if they ask me. What I thought I'd do is—"

But Yolanda was pawing the ground.

"Another time, uncle darling. We've got heaps and heaps to do. We must go. We had to come and tell Mrs. Merrion, and we've told her. Come along."

They refused a lift. They walked to the gate, and then the Professor stopped and came hurrying back.

"Quite forgot," he said to Mrs. Merrion. "Meant to ask if Esmond brought over my reading glasses."

"Oh, yes—he did. I quite forgot to tell you," Mrs. Merrion said. "Paul, will you fetch them? I put them on the hall table."

Paul stepped into the hall and came back with the case.

"Thanks. Haven't needed them, fortunately, but can't be without them," the Professor explained. "Had to put them on to study that bit of paper of Esmond's. Didn't know he went in for that kind of thing."

"What kind of thing?" Paul asked.

"Oriental languages. My department, I would have said. Good-bye, good-bye."

He hurried after Yolanda. Paul looked at his mother.

"Oriental languages?" he repeated. "What bit of paper?"

"I wasn't there. The Professor and I were walking away from the cottage when Esmond called him back and asked him if he'd look at something. I walked on. You're looking puzzled—is this something important?"

"I don't suppose so. I shan't be in to lunch. Lydia says she wants to think, so I'm taking her out to give her some fresh air to think in."

He drove her to a village—Paul thought it must be one of the smallest in England—which had a duck pond, a miniature village green and a small, thatched-roof building which proclaimed itself the Coaching Inn. But even this picturesque background did not rouse Paul from the reverie in which he had been lost throughout the drive. Lydia waited until they were inside the Inn, seated in a tiny parlour, waiting for their lunch, before asking him what was the matter.

"Nothing much. I'm just thinking," he answered.

"I was the one who was supposed to do the thinking. Are you thinking the same things as I'm thinking?"

"I've only got one idea—it's going round and round."

"I've got several ideas; they're going round each other," she told him. "Couldn't we pool our preoccupations?"

"I haven't got anything to pool. All I'm certain of is that there's something funny going on, only I don't know what it is. I think someone's after bricks. They're not after all the bricks, only some of the bricks. But which bricks are they choosing, and what good can bricks do them?"

He got up, went to the bar and came back with drinks.

"No cider," he said. "At least, no special cider—only this stuff out of a bottle. Will it do?"

"Yes. Thank you. Go on with what you were saying."

"No. I've got a suggestion. Let's cut out ideas and intuition and all the rest of it, and see if we can assemble some hard facts and see where they lead."

"I think there's—"

"No thinks. Hard facts, I said. We want to get to the bottom of why someone took bricks from my grandmother's kitchen garden and from your stepfather's garden—right?"

"Yes. Why did they?"

"Where did this brick business first begin?"

"In the tower."

"Which gradually shed its bricks. From time to time, people from the town, people who wanted to save money, or people with an eye for a good-looking brick, came up the hill and helped themselves to all the bricks they wanted. But when my grandmother started to build her house, there were still bricks left. The lower part of the tower was still standing."

"I don't see—"

"I don't see, either—yet. So let's proceed. It was Dudley Roach who spotted that the bricks were unusual. To whom did he mention the fact?"

"To your grandmother. And to us all when he came to dinner at your mother's house."

"And in mentioning them, did he say anything about inscriptions?"

"I said your grandmother shouldn't have sent my stepfather a bill for the bricks that were scratched. Dudley said something about inscriptions, or perhaps what he said was that the scratches were builders' marks. But nobody took much notice."

"Oh yes, somebody did. Next point: Would your stepfather be able to remember whether any of the sundial bricks had scratches? And next, and most important: why did the Professor have to put on his glasses?"

"To read something. Something on a piece of paper. That's nothing to do with bricks."

"You think not? I don't agree. Last of all: we have to find the Professor and ask him what was on that paper.

When we get answers to those puzzles, we'll see where we are. Are you with me as far as I've gone?"

"I think so. But I can think better when I've eaten."

"Then you differ from the rest of mankind. If you want a clear brain you need an empty stomach. Shakespeare said so, though not in those exact words."

They were told that their meal was ready, but they did not have to move; a cloth was spread on the table in the parlour and lunch was brought to them. It was not the rich fare of the day before; it was a cold meal, slices of cold lamb, ham cut thickly, pickled onions in an enormous jar, bread and cheese. Paul, watching Lydia, thought that she was the right kind of girl to take out to meals: hungry, appreciative--and unfussy.

It was not until the table had been cleared that they spoke again of bricks.

"What you were saying," she told Paul, "is that some of the bricks had an inscription on them, and your uncle copied something onto a piece of paper and showed it to the Professor, who said it was an Oriental language."

"You were right about needing a full stomach. And you're right as far as you've gone in your summing-up."

"But . . ."

"But what?"

"I don't see any connection between Oriental languages and the bricks."

"You didn't eat enough. Who built that tower?"

"Oh, I see—a man from the East."

"You make it sound like a Nativity play. But it wasn't the man from the East who built the tower. It was his wife, his mistress, his Indian princess."

"You mean she put an inscription on some of the bricks of the tower?"

"I do."

"What for?"

"Use your head. Or better still, use some of the imagination you showed when you first cooked up the story of Exerton's release from prison. It's always been assumed that his loot, whatever his loot was, if there was any loot, went into the river with the coach. But suppose it wasn't Exerton who had the loot or treasure? Suppose it was the woman? She builds his stone house—but with all those workmen round, where could she hide the treasure?"

"In the tower?"

"No. There was nothing in or under the tower."

"If there wasn't anything in the tower or under the tower, what was the point of building it?"

"Didn't you say that Exerton was in prison?"

"Yes. Oh, I see now. She thought that at any moment, the authorities might come and get her, too?"

"She was without doubt implicated in whatever jiggery-pokery Exerton had been up to. So she built a tower. Not a high tower; she wanted it within her reach, so that she could make the grooves and scratches on the bricks. I don't know what language she used, but it was one she'd feel certain wouldn't be generally known. There couldn't have been many professors of Oriental studies in Ellstream at that time."

"But if we can work out a theory, then—"

"Then it's obvious that my uncle has been working one out, too. The more the day advances, the more certain I feel that he's got as far as we've got. In fact, he's several steps ahead."

"Then why hasn't he said anything about it?"

"Because he must have made up his mind to try and find out what the bricks said. If those inscriptions could be made to form a consecutive pattern, he's home."

She stared at him.

"I don't believe it," she said slowly. "I can't believe it."

"That's because you don't know him as I do."

"He wouldn't. If he took those bricks, and knew that my stepfather had been blamed—"

"He didn't know that when he took them."

"He knew afterwards."

"Yes. And said nothing."

"I can't believe it."

"You don't want to believe it. Nor do I. You were with him twice in town—didn't he drop any hint about this?"

"I didn't see much of him yesterday."

"But you went into town with him."

"We went down together, but then he said he had a lot to do, and I didn't see him again until I met him just before we both met Dudley Roach. Then we went round looking at the bricks in the town that Dudley knew about."

"Did Esmond have any parcels with him?"

"No."

"So he hadn't done any shopping. And he's gone off on his own today. I wonder where he is?"

"You really, honestly think there's something in what we've been saying?"

"All I believe is that the wife might have left a message for Exerton. A lifetime in the East India Company meant, in those days, that a man wouldn't come back to England empty-handed. Abuses, bribes, malpractices—it was the heyday for men who wanted to make a fortune the fast way."

"What would they bring home—money?"

"No. That is, money in some other form. My guess would be diamonds. And if those bricks had an inscription on them; if the inscription indicated the place in which the wife had hidden the diamonds or whatever; if my uncle picked up the scent and has been following it, he won't give up until he's located whatever it was. Why?

196

One reason will be because if there's loot, it'll be on my grandmother's land, and he'll feel entitled to it."

"He's the eldest son; it would have been his anyway, in time."

"No, it wouldn't. Do you suppose she would have left him anything when she died? Haven't you realized yet how deeply they hate one another?" He looked at the large, round, old-fashioned clock ticking loudly on the wall. "Time to go. We've got a lot to do."

He paid the bill and they walked into the stone-floored hall. Paul opened the front door, and a gust of wind brought in a spatter of raindrops.

"We'll run for it," he said, and they ran. As they drove away, the shower turned to a steady downpour.

"Where do we go now?" she asked.

"Home."

"Yours or mine?"

"Mine."

"Are you going to tell your mother anything about this?"

"No. Most certainly not. We've made up a fairy story for our own amusement. If we ever read it aloud to anybody, it'll be to my uncle, and then we'll ask him to give us his version. But we're only halfway through it."

Mrs. Merrion was having tea. They joined her, and Paul fetched from the kitchen cakes, biscuits and scones.

"Lydia hasn't had a thing since lunch," he told his mother. "About this morning: you heard what the Professor said about the paper Esmond showed him?"

"Yes."

"You didn't see the size of the paper, or the kind of paper, by any chance?"

"No. It was in the cottage. I came without waiting for the Professor. He wasn't long looking at it."

"Do you know if Esmond's back from town?"

"He isn't coming back until tonight. He rang up to say he'd met some friends and was going to join them for dinner." She paused, frowning. "You don't think, do you . . . ?"

"That he'll borrow money from them, and you'll have to pay it back? Somehow, I don't think he's borrowing money." He looked at Lydia. "If you're ready, we'll go."

They thanked Mrs. Merrion and went out to the car. But when they drove out to the road, Paul did not turn towards Mr. Ainstey's house.

"Where?" Lydia asked.

"To town, to see if we can find Esmond."

They did not find him. But they found, seated side by side on a bench at the Plough, the Professor and Dudley Roach. The younger man was looking gloomy, but the Professor was in the best of spirits.

"Sit down, sit down. You must have some of this excellent cider," he told Paul and Lydia. "I am trying to cheer up this young man. I am trying to convince him that my niece is not as bad as he imagines."

"I didn't say anything about bad. I denied your claim to her having a softer side to her nature. What do we want with a riding school? She'll worm her way into the lives of the masters, beginning with me." He drank deep. "Ending with me, if I don't watch out."

"She is a nice girl," said the Professor earnestly. "It's just one of those cases in which the child is misdirected by a parent. Her father is a nonentity, like me. Her mother taught Yolanda to assert herself. To fail to assert oneself meant being pushed into a corner and overlooked. I am certain that my niece has some of my nature—a little. So if she meets anybody who puts her into a corner, she will find the position less unpleasant than her mother led her to believe." He finished his cider and shook his head when

Dudley made a move to order more. "No, no, no, thank you. I must go. If you're not going back yet, Paul, I shall ask you to get me a taxi."

"I'll take you up. I'm taking Lydia home," Paul said.

The Professor paused to address a final word to Dudley.

"Good-bye, young man. If you can quell a classroom full of today's little boys, I do not fear for you. You will be all right. Good-bye."

When he was settled in the car, Lydia asked him a question.

"Were you comforting Mr. Roach?"

"I was reassuring him. He is apprehensive, and with good reason—though I did not tell him that. You must have observed that Yolanda is, of all things, single-minded. She has never before shown the smallest interest in a man. It was horses, horses and more horses. Now it is Dudley, Dudley and more Dudley. I don't think he will escape, and I don't think it will be a bad thing for either of them. He is worried at the moment, and has lost a little of his spirit. She will go too far in some way—she will irritate him, or try to bully him, and then he will turn on her. I don't think, from the little I have seen of him, that anybody will ever rule Mr. Roach."

"I agree," Lydia said, and the Professor turned to her gratefully.

"Now *you* have reassured *me,*" he said. "Thank you."

Paul stopped the car at his grandmother's gate. The Professor got out and thanked him for the lift.

"You're welcome," Paul said. "Don't go for a minute. I'd like to ask you something."

"Well?"

"I was puzzled when you said that my uncle was showing an interest in Oriental languages. You said that was your department."

"Oh well, you know, that was my little joke. But I was

rather surprised to see that sketch he'd made—he said he'd come across an inscription, or a part of one, and was wondering whether it had any meaning or not. Well, there wasn't much for me to go on, but what there was was easy enough to identify, even to decipher. I asked Esmond if he had any more of it, and he said he hadn't, and had only shown this to me because it might, as he expressed it, be up my street. Which of course it was."

"What was it?" Lydia asked.

"Just part of an inscription, that's all," the Professor answered. "He had no idea what the language was, or even if it was a language. I was able to give him confirmation."

He had turned away when Paul spoke again.

"What language was it?" he asked.

The Professor, without pausing, spoke over his shoulder.

"That was the interesting part. It was Sanskrit." He stopped, turned and came back to the car. "The old sacred language of India," he explained. "Most Hindu literature, you know, is written in Sanskrit. It's a far richer language than Greek or Latin. It has eight cases, and those include an instrumental and a locative. The power of making compound words is almost unlimited. The importance of Sanskrit is that it's a— I'm afraid I'm keeping you, but it's always unwise to get a person on to his own subject. There was no time to tell Esmond much about the use of hymns and the nature of the ritual and so on. All I could do was advise him to go down to the library in the town, which I'm told has a very good reading room. Most libraries will be able to produce at least something about Sanskrit, and all Esmond wanted, so he told me, was to see what Sanskrit characters looked like, so that if ever he happened to come across any further examples, he could at least identify them. But perhaps he lost interest?"

"No, I don't think he lost interest," Paul said. "Thank you for clearing up the point."

He drove away. Neither he nor Lydia spoke again until he stopped at Mr. Ainstey's door. Then:

"The library," Paul said slowly. "The one place we didn't think of looking. The reading room of the library, where he's been hidden, studying Sanskrit characters to find out what was inscribed on those bricks. We—you—made up a fairy tale, but it's turning out to be a real tale, with no fairies." He turned to her. "How does it feel to be a detective?"

"You're the detective. I'm a reporter."

"Would the reporter care to have dinner in town with the detective?"

She smiled.

"That's nice of you, but I think I'd like to stay at home tonight. I shan't be able to do anything to comfort my stepfather, but he might feel like talking to someone, and he'd rather talk to me than talk to my aunt. Thanks all the same."

She got out of the car and he raised a hand in leave-taking.

"I'll be round early tomorrow morning," he told her, "and we'll go over together to the cottage and have a little talk with Esmond."

It was a plan which was never put into operation.

Chapter
Eleven

THE TELEPHONE IN Mrs. Merrion's hall rang that night as Paul was on his way up to bed. He turned automatically to go down and answer it, and then paused, remembering that it was close on midnight. He felt certain that nobody in Ellstream would telephone at this hour. London? Or—he went slowly down the stairs and picked up the receiver—Venice?

It was Lydia's voice. He drew a long breath of relief.

"Paul? Lydia here. Look, perhaps I shouldn't have—"

"What's wrong?"

"Nothing. Only I thought I ought to tell you . . ."

"Well, go on; tell me."

"I stayed up late, reading. When I put out my light and drew my curtains . . . Did you know that I'm in my mother's room, which overlooks the garden and the cottage?"

"No. Go on."

"I think your uncle has gone."

"Gone?" he echoed blankly. "Gone where?"

"Well, just gone. There was a light in the cottage when I drew back my curtains. It went out and I saw him come out, and I was surprised, so I stood and watched him. All he did was shut the door behind him, and walk away—but he was carrying his briefcase, and he told me once that that was all his luggage, so I thought I ought to tell you in case—"

"Are you dressed?"

"No. It wouldn't take long to put something on."

"Then put something on and meet me at the cottage. How long ago did you see him?"

"About twenty minutes. I couldn't ring before because my stepfather was in his study, and would have heard me, so I waited until he went to bed."

"Pity. Will you hurry?"

They met outside the cottage, which was in darkness. Paul tried the door and found it unlocked.

"Come on," he said.

They went in. Paul switched on a light and they stood looking round the room. A cup and saucer had been washed and left to drain on the kitchen sink. The bed-clothes were neatly folded, the sheets on a chair ready for laundering, the blankets piled on the bed. A half-empty bottle of brandy stood in the middle of the living room table, and under it was a note in Esmond's handwriting, with two scrawled lines:

"Called away. Many, many thanks. Back some day."

Paul raised his head and spoke slowly.

"He found it—whatever it was," he said. "He found it, and he's gone, taking it with him. You and I were very clever to do our detective homework so well, but we did it too slowly. We took too long. He was two paces ahead of us all the way."

"You can't be sure that he found anything. I mean, you

204

can't be sure that he found anything here. He may have deciphered the inscription and discovered that whatever it was was in London—or somewhere else. Perhaps he's gone to find it."

"I'd stake anything—"

He broke off abruptly, walked to the small storeroom and threw open the door. Switching on the light, he called to Lydia.

"Come in here."

She came and stood beside him, and looked where he was looking—at a line of bricks that had been placed on the floor against the wall, bricks set end to end, each one bearing characters. They gazed for a time in silence, and then Paul spoke.

"There it is," he said. "The whole story, told on bricks. He scented a mystery—the word inscription was enough. He stole the marked bricks, he sorted them, he spread them out, he copied the inscriptions and then went down to the library and deciphered as much as he needed to decipher. He left the bricks here for us to do the same—if we want to. The fact that he's left the evidence for all to see proves that he's got whatever there was to get." He turned to her. "Do you want to try and find out the end of the story?"

"If we can, yes. But how?"

"By going up to my grandmother's. The answer's somewhere in her grounds. All we can do is go up there and take a look round. If he dug anywhere, we'll see the marks. We'll walk up; I can't get my car out without waking my mother, and I'd like to keep this strictly between you and me. Have you got decent shoes on? It'll be rough going. You brought a torch?"

"Yes. Only a small one."

"It'll do. Let's go."

He had been right about the rough going, she found

almost at once; as they left Mrs. Merrion's property and crossed to the heath-like territory that bordered Lady Charlotte's, she found herself constantly stumbling. Heath became woodland. The torches they carried gave no more than a pinpoint of light, insufficient to show them the roots and stones that lay on the path.

"It's a lot of land," Lydia said after a time. "We can't tramp over the whole of it, can we?"

"We won't have to, if my guess is correct."

"What guess?"

"There's only one thing on this property that was on it when my grandmother began to build. A statue. A small bronze Hermes. She left it where it was. I'm going to make for it and see if there's anything to be seen. The idea must have occurred to Esmond."

"With hundreds of trees to bury things under, why would anybody choose to dig near a statue?" she asked in bewilderment.

"Trees fall down. Trees die. Trees get struck by lightning. A bronze statue on a stone plinth seems to me a good landmark and an enduring one. It may be a silly idea and it may be wrong, but as I said, it must have occurred to Esmond."

"I don't understand why he went away. Nobody would have suspected him."

"Except us. He knew we'd got our noses to the ground. He didn't hide those bricks he lined up in the storeroom; if there are any traces near the statue, he'll have left them for anybody to find."

"But—"

"Put out your torch. From now on we'll be on the drive, and anybody looking out of a window will see the light. Hang on to me and try not to make a noise. It's a still night, and sounds will carry."

They went on silently, but they were now moving more

swiftly. The clouds parted for a moment and their way was clear in the moonlight—then they were in darkness again. But Lydia had had time to see the widening of the drive, and a dark object at its center.

When they were almost up to the statue, Paul put out a hand and halted her. Then he led her round until they stood with their backs to the house.

"Now," he said.

He switched on his torch. Then he drew a deep breath.

"It's nice to be right sometimes," he said quietly.

They were looking at the statue, but it was not on its plinth. It had been lifted off and placed on the drive. Below the place on which it had stood was a small, square cavity. It was empty.

They drew near and looked inside it. The square hollowed out of the plinth had been completely covered by the base of the statue; it was clean and quite dry.

"We needn't go to the trouble of trying to find out what was on those bricks," Paul said. "The inscription was *Lift up the statue of Hermes and under it you will find our treasure safely hidden.* But he didn't find it. Esmond found it. And we'll never know if the Indian princess arranged a hiding place because she was afraid the law was on her track—or because she knew she wouldn't live long enough to see Exerton when he got out of prison. She obviously didn't want to risk putting anything down on paper, but she must have been quite certain that he'd go into the tower and—"

"—get the message."

"Yes. It was a clever idea of hers to leave a message that nobody but Exerton could have deciphered."

Lydia spoke in a puzzled voice.

"But if your grandmother had decided to move the statue—"

"She would have found whatever there was to find. But

she didn't move it. One day, perhaps, in the very distant future, Esmond might tell us what he found under it."

"Why didn't he put the statue back on its plinth? If he could lift it down, he could put it back, and then nobody would have known that—"

"He didn't put it back because he wanted his mother to find it lying here. He wanted her to see that hiding place."

"Why?"

"Because never, since they had their final row, has he ever succeeded in getting anything out of her. She repudiated his debts. She cut him out of her Will. She saw to it, as far as she was able, that he'd get no help of any kind from anybody over whom she had any influence. When she sees the statue off its plinth, when she sees this cavity, she'll know he's got something—something of considerable value, or why would anybody go to such lengths to hide it? She'll know he's got it, but she'll never know what it was. He's left her a nice little problem to work on whenever she can't sleep at night."

"You're not going to leave the statue where it is, are you?"

"Of course I am. That's what Esmond wanted."

"I know. You've just explained why. But please put it back. Please. He's got what he needed; he'll be all right —so why not let it go at that? If you put the statue back, nobody need ever know, except us, and it'll be a better end to the story than letting him use it to get his own back on his mother. You told me that he's been doing just that for a good many years. So put the statue back and then we can go and throw those bricks out of the cottage, and nobody'll know there was any inscription. Then it can all be forgotten."

"Is that how you'd do it?"

"Yes. It's not my business, but there's enough meanness in the world without making any more. She's an old woman, and he's had his revenge. Put the statue back. If you change your mind later, you can always come out on some dark night and lift it off again. Do you want any help, or can you do it alone?"

"If my middle-aged uncle could manage it, why can't I?"

She watched him struggle. Breathless after his third attempt to lift the statue, he addressed her irritably.

"It was easy enough to lift the damn thing down. It's getting it off the ground that's the trouble. I ought to make you do it—it was your idea."

He bent, and this time came up clasping the Hermes. He placed it on the plinth and moved it until its base was once more over the cavity. Then he walked round smoothing the gravel on the drive to efface the marks left on it. Lydia spoke out of the darkness.

"The other name for Hermes is Mercury, isn't it?"

"You know about Hermes, as well as about Haydn?"

"Only his name."

"In Roman mythology he was Mercury, the god of trade. In Greek mythology he was the son of Zeus and— wait for it—the patron saint of thieves. Do you suppose Esmond remembered that when he was lifting him off his plinth?"

"Wasn't Mercury a messenger?"

"He was. Zeus made him his messenger and ambassador, and he was commissioned, among other things, to slay the hundred-eyed Argus and carry the infant Bacchus to the nymphs at Nysa. He was also the god of good fortune—perhaps that's what Esmond remembered. If you could see Esmond now, perhaps he'd be wearing winged sandals."

"I wonder where they'll carry him?"

They left Hermes-Mercury and went back to the cottage. They carried the bricks outside and left them lying in heaps in the wood. Then Lydia dusted her hands and gave a sigh of relief.

"I'm glad I don't have to work night shifts," she said. "Can I go home now?"

"Yes. Thanks." He hesitated, and then came up to her and took one of her hands. "In fact," he said, "thanks for everything."

"How much is everything?"

"Well, for being here. For ... for everything. That doesn't cover it, but I'd like you to know that I'm grateful."

It was easy to work that out, she thought. Thanks for being here and helping him to fill in time. Thanks for contributing whatever it was she'd contributed to turn him from the morose individual she had seen on the station on her arrival, to the untroubled-seeming man he had shown himself for the past couple of days. If it came to that, she had some thanks to offer.

"I've enjoyed tailing Esmond," she said.

She tried to draw her hand away, but he held it fast.

"Lydia—"

She waited. But there was no more. He lifted her hand and laid it for a moment against his cheek, and then released it.

"Not yet," he said quietly. "Soon. Good night."

When she opened the side door of the house, she turned and saw him standing where she had left him. She raised a hand, went inside and crept soundlessly to her room. She undressed, got into bed and lay examining her feelings. She did not have to examine them closely; she knew only too well what they were. How much did he feel for her? There was response—of that she was certain. How strong or how deep it was, she could not guess. What did "soon" mean? "Not yet"—that was clear enough; he was not yet free. If and when that other girl returned ...

She slept, but not well. She was glad to see daylight filling the room.

She hoped that he would come to the house during the morning, but there was no sign of him. She lunched with Brenda, and while they were eating, the telegram came. It was telephoned from the post office, and Brenda took it down and brought it to Lydia.

"Return, all is forgiven," she said, and handed her the paper on which she had written the message. "You've got your job back."

Lydia read. Mr. Kellerman was back. The quartet was to play in Plymouth the day after tomorrow.

"That means leaving almost at once, doesn't it?" Brenda asked.

"Yes. I ought to go on the evening train."

Something in her voice made Brenda's eyes rest on her uneasily.

"I daresay you'll be glad to get back to London."

"I'm glad about the job. But I was enjoying myself here."

"I haven't done much to help you to enjoy yourself. Though with robberies and threats of police and so on, it can't have been as dull for you as it might have been."

"No, it hasn't been dull."

She rose and began to clear away the plates.

"You can leave those," Brenda said. "I'm going to make some coffee."

"Not for me, thanks. I'd like to go over and tell Paul about the job."

Brenda's eyes widened, but she said nothing. She made coffee for herself, her thoughts elsewhere. She heard Lydia go out, and paused in mid-kitchen with the coffee pot in her hand, a frown on her forehead.

"I hope," she said aloud, "she knows what she's doing."

Lydia knew what she was doing: she was going to see

211

Paul, to tell him that Mr. Kellerman was back and that she was leaving Ellstream this evening. She wanted him to know, because when he knew, she would know whether he wanted to see her again. He must, she thought, say something, however vague, about meeting her, seeing her, running into her when he went back to London. If he didn't . . . well, it would be better, in a way, to know that it was over. In a way.

His car was not on the drive, but that did not mean that he was out; it might be in the garage, or round the other side of the house. There was no sign of anybody in the garden. She walked to the front door, but before she reached it, it was opened by Mrs. Merrion.

"Come in, Lydia." She led the way to the garden room. "Do sit down, won't you?"

"I can't stay, thank you. I just came to . . . Is Paul in?"

"No. He—"

"It doesn't matter. When he comes in, would you tell him that I've got my job back?"

"The quartet has started again?"

"Yes. I've got to go back to London this evening. If I don't see you again . . . Perhaps if you ever came up to London, we could meet?"

"I'd like that very much. Wait a moment while I write down your address."

She turned to the desk and noted it on a pad. It seemed to Lydia that having written it, there was a very long pause before she turned once more to face her. She seemed about to speak, but there was only silence.

"Is Paul . . . did he go into town?" she asked.

"No. He—" Mrs. Merrion made a visible effort. "As a matter of fact, Lydia, he . . . he's gone away."

The silence, which had been merely awkward, was now painful. But for the life of her, Lydia could not break it. At last she heard herself speaking.

"Gone away?"

"Yes."

"When?"

"Early this morning. He drove straight to London airport."

"Airport?"

"Yes. He's gone to Venice."

Chapter
Twelve

Mrs. KELLERMAN, SUPERVISING the rehearsal on the day after Lydia's return to London, gave her a brief account of Mr. Kellerman's reasons for returning, and added her own reasons for believing that he would soon vanish again.

"The money," she explained, in the German-English which twenty years of British citizenship had not eradicated in herself or her husband, "the money, only the money, Lydia, my child. He took the money and together they spent it and when it is gone, he is back mit us. Soon there will be more—never did I stop to make engagements for the quartet. There will be more money, and another woman, and he will go. It is like that."

Lydia, looking across her music stand at the broad, shrewd countenance, felt a stir of admiration. There had been no break in the quartet's series of engagements; some of them Mrs. Kellerman had had to cancel, pleading the illness of her husband, but she had continued her work of manager for the team, and the quartet had engagements that would take them to the end of September. After Plymouth, they were to play in Stratford; from Stratford they were to go to Bath, and then back to London.

It was after the concert they gave on their return, in a draughty hall in Chelsea, that they were mentioned for the first time by the press. Lydia, after reading the four lines, unfortunately showed them to Mr. Kellerman. He was standing at the end of the platform on which they were to perform that evening—an annual engagement for which they always agreed to take a lower fee, as the proceeds of the concert were to be given to charity. He read the notice aloud in a choked voice, squeezed the paper against his chest and called wildly for his wife.

"Mama! Greta, come! See what I haf!" He tripped, lost his balance and fell down the four steps that led down to the auditorium, got to his feet and ran stumbling down the aisle to find his wife.

Lydia, watching him, knew that a month ago, she would have shared his sense of triumph. But her mind, in the past so intent, so absorbed in the quartet and the concerts, now seemed to have developed a disconcerting tendency to wander away to unrelated matters—matters, moreover, on which she had decided it was better not to dwell.

She had been glad to get back to work—not only to work, but also to London, even to her room at Mrs. Lyle's. In the brief time she had been away, a change had come over the city; foreigners were everywhere, the shops were crowded, the parks thronged. Ellstream seemed a very long way away, and it appeared that Providence was aiding her to forget the place and all that had happened there, for on her return there had been no Greek girl in the kitchen to give her news of clients. She had, Mrs. Lyle explained, run into a little trouble over a work permit, and had departed in a hurry. But she had not been needed to relay the news, for at the end of June, there it was for all to read: Paul Esmond, son of: Diana Audrey, daughter of. They were to be married, and no doubt they would go to Venice for their honeymoon, since it held so many memories for them both.

It was not only the announcement of the engagement that had given her mind this tendency to wander; it was her recurrent longing to know just what she had said, or done, when Mrs. Merrion had informed her of Paul's departure to Venice. Between that moment, and finding herself back at her stepfather's house, there was a blank which she would dearly have liked to fill. She hoped, prayed that she had behaved naturally. Naturally? No, not naturally. To have behaved naturally would have been to give a loud wail of realization and loss. She had probably uttered some kind of polite sentence and said good-bye and got herself out of the house without giving herself away—and now she could be grateful that she was settling down to life as she had lived it before going to Ellstream.

Settling . . . but not yet settled. Unsettling things happened at intervals. Two days after she had read the announcement of the engagement, the post had brought her a small package. Inside was a silver figurine, four inches high. Hermes. And two weeks later, when she had convinced herself that it had been sent as a token of farewell, there came a tiny silver tower. No card, no message; the postmark London. And in July, the tiny silver brick.

Most unsettling of all was her impression, one night at a concert in mid-August, that Paul Merrion was in the audience. He was too far away for her to be sure. If it was Paul Merrion, why had he come alone? There was no message, and he did not come round after the performance. But he was at the next concert—and the next.

The room once occupied by the Greek girl had been taken by a young artist. Finding it too far from the Art School, he left, and was succeeded by an elderly widow who spoke little and cooked herself two large meals a day. Her objections to Lydia's practising mounted until she said she could stand it no longer, and gave notice. When the married couple who followed her found the room too small, and departed, Lydia went upstairs and after some hard bargaining with Mrs. Lyle, arranged to take the room herself. She turned it into a living room, and used the intervals between concerts for painting walls and doors, attending sales and making herself a home. The result was so unexpectedly successful that she began to invite friends to supper; her spirits rose slightly. She was no longer a bed-sitter; she was a woman with an apartment of her own, with a private entrance—the area steps. Her salary had increased and would go on increasing, for the press notices had grown warmer and Mrs. Kellerman had grown bolder and asked higher and higher fees. The receipts were no longer kept in a cash box which her husband could carry away; they were securely banked in her name, and if he wanted money, he was obliged to tell her why.

No news had appeared in the papers about Paul Merrion's wedding. Lydia's mother, not surprisingly, made no mention of him in her letters; Brenda never wrote. There was no bridge to link him with the life she was leading now.

Until there came, in the first week of September, a letter from Mrs. Merrion. She was, she wrote, coming up to London to do some shopping; would Lydia be free to meet her for lunch on the ninth? At Franzero's. One o'clock?

Lydia wrote several letters of acceptance, tore up seven and posted the eighth; yes, she would be free and she would love to be at Franzero's at one o'clock on the ninth.

Mrs. Merrion, waiting for her at the bar, watched her enter and saw heads turn to look at her. There it was, she thought, the quality she had noted on their first meeting. Simplicity. Good looks that didn't amount to beauty, but a lovely figure, a graceful carriage and a look of— there was no other word, even in the hubbub of Franzero's—serenity.

Their table had been reserved; there was time for a drink if Lydia would like one. But Lydia preferred to go straight in to lunch, thus leaving, she said, more time for Mrs. Merrion to do her shopping afterwards.

They sat down. The first ten minutes went in looking down the meter-long menu and finally disregarding every item but two: a grilled sole and a green salad for Mrs. Merrion, pizza and a mixed salad for Lydia. Wine? Was there any cider? Lydia asked; she would prefer that.

"Sure that's all you want?" Mrs. Merrion asked, giving up her menu.

"Yes, that's all. Thank you."

"I rang up your mother and told her I was meeting you today. She sent her love. I suppose she keeps you in touch with Ellstream gossip?"

"No. Is Yolanda still there?"

"Very much so. She's quite extraordinary. Everybody knows she's madly in love with Dudley Roach—except Yolanda. She's marching straight to her goal, all the same. She's living with the Maths master and his wife in one of those houses just below the school."

"And the riding school?"

"Flourishing. At least, it flourished last term and I daresay there'll be even more riders when the boys go back after the holidays." A brief pause. "Paul couldn't join us for lunch because he said he'd be given lunch on the plane—he's just back from Stockholm, where he went on Bank business."

The mention of his name was unexpected, the news of his activities inexplicable. Lydia summoned her courage and put a question.

"His marriage . . . ?"

Mrs. Merrion smiled.

"Off. Thank God, that's finished at last. You saw the announcement of his engagement?"

"Yes."

"Mrs. Framley's first attempt to pin him down. I can't tell you anything about it, because I'm under strict orders from Paul to let him do the explaining. My job was to get you here."

Lydia, in a daze, saw the waiter place something before her, and with an effort, recognized it as the pizza she had ordered. She discovered that her appetite, since her return from Ellstream capricious, had returned and was intent on making up for lost time. Having at first refused cheese, she changed her mind and asked for it. The waiter, father of a growing family, watched her and hinted that the charlotte russe was always particularly good here; she said that she would like some.

They had ordered coffee and Mrs. Merrion had finished hers before Paul appeared. Lydia, facing the entrance, saw him standing in the doorway looking round the tables; then he saw her and began to move towards her.

"Paul," she told his mother.

"About time, too," Mrs. Merrion told him as he reached them and pulled out a chair. "I've got hours more shopping to do."

He turned to look at Lydia. For the first time since his entrance, he smiled.

"Hello," he said.

"Hello."

Mrs. Merrion rose.

"I'm going to leave you two to talk," she said. "No, Paul, don't come with me; I'll get a taxi. Lydia, we'll meet again soon."

Paul went with her to the street, returned and took the chair she had vacated.

"Had enough to eat?" he asked.

"Yes. Thank you."

"Then shall we go? I've got a lot to say, and I'd like to say it in quieter surroundings."

They walked to his car. She began to give him directions, and he stopped her.

"I know your house," he said. "I've been there."

"To the house?"

"To the house. Didn't you tell me to inform myself as to how the other half lived? I saw a notice about a vacant room in a front window. I knocked. I was admitted. I was shown the vacant room and the kitchen. I informed the landlady that I would consider becoming an inmate only if she agreed to redecorate the room and the kitchen, put in a new stove, install a dish-washing machine and wall-to-wall carpeting, and call in the builders to turn the so-called garden into a bathroom. The interview ended."

He brought the car to a stop outside the house. She led him down, opened the door and ushered him into the narrow passage that was now carpeted in dark green, with walls painted in a lighter shade. The kitchen was pale blue and white. The tour of the apartment ended with her making tea and carrying it into the living room.

"Now you can talk," she told him. "Beginning with an explanation of why you went to Venice without saying good-bye."

"What could I have said? I went to Venice to wind up some unfinished business—but I didn't know how long it was going to take me to end it, and I was certain that before it ended, I was going to be involved in hostilities. I was right. When I came back to England, the one thing I was determined to do was keep you out of the mess. I wanted to keep away from you until I was clear of all entanglement. If you think these past months have been pleasant, you're mistaken, but I suppose I can write it all off as experience. In a few years, I'll tell you the sordid details, but for the moment I prefer to forget them. Did you really think, when you heard that I'd gone to Venice, that I was leaving you behind?"

"Yes."

"Was I wrong when I thought, at Ellstream, that something had grown up between us? Something deep? I don't think I was. I went away certain that you felt as I felt. Later, the feeling grew shaky. It wasn't until I talked to my mother that I found myself on solid ground again. After listening to her, I knew it was all right."

"What was all right?"

"Us. You and me. Yourself, myself. Because I knew for certain how you felt." He took her hand and pulled her down to sit beside him. "After hearing my mother's opinion, I felt safe."

She spoke in bewilderment.

"But I didn't tell your mother anything about how I felt."

"No?" He laughed. "You told her all she wanted to know—and all I wanted to know."

"I simply asked her where you were, and she said you'd gone to Venice."

"And you were standing beside her desk when she told you. You didn't say anything. You picked up a bill that was lying on the desk—the bill for the new curtains she'd put in my room. You tore it into very small pieces, very slowly and painstakingly. When you'd reduced the bill to confetti, you laid the bits very carefully on the desk—and

222

went home. Without a word. Without even saying good-bye. She thought that indicated a certain—"

"I did that?"

"You did rather more than that. One tear—one only —trickled slowly down one cheek—one only. My mother and I agreed that this indicated a certain—"

"There was a blank. Sometimes I wondered what I'd said or done. Thank you for the Hermes and the tower and—"

"Those were to remind you. They were to remind you of Ellstream, and of what happened there."

"Going to concerts—did you do that to remind me, too?"

"I didn't attend as a music lover. I went because I wanted to see you. And not only to see you—to keep an eye on you. I sat in my car after the performances, with a view of the stage door, to assure myself that you didn't go home with anybody I didn't like the look of. I didn't want you stolen from me by some lout of a cello player. I wanted to see you, and to see what you were doing—but I couldn't claim you until I was free. Do you understand that?"

"Yes. But—"

"But you thought I was going to be married. So I am, but only when you say so. All I ask, for the moment, is to be with you. When we're not working, we've got to be together. I've been storm-tossed and I want to lie up in harbour. If ever a man needed a restful woman like yourself, it's myself at this present time. I want to rest —and refit. And while I'm doing that, we'll discuss how and where we'll be married."

"I wish Esmond could come."

"Never mind about Esmond. Will you come closer? I can't embrace you across a chasm, and I've just remembered that I've never made you a formal proposal. But first things first: Lydia Cresset, do you love me?"

"Yes."

"I love you very much. Now we come to the hard part. Will you marry me?"

"Yes. Thank you."

Mrs. Ainstey, on being informed some time later of her youngest daughter's engagement, felt momentary surprise which was almost at once succeeded by the conviction that however gratifying a union this might be from the material point of view, a lovely girl like Lydia deserved the best. Paul Merrion was lucky to get her.

She went in search of her husband; he would be very pleased, she thought; he had more than once said that it was time Lydia was married. She found him in the garden.

"Have you got a moment, George? I'd like to tell you a piece of news."

He leaned on the hoe.

"Good news?"

"Very good. I've just had a letter from Lydia."

"Oh. What's she got to say?"

"She's engaged. She—"

"Engaged?"

"Yes."

"Engaged to be married, you mean?"

"Yes. She's—"

"About time. But if I were you, I'd wait a bit before you start ringing bells. Next thing you know, she might be writing to say it's all off. She showed no signs of settling down when she was here in May."

"But we're into November now; she's had months in which to decide whether she really liked him or not. I wish I'd been here during her visit; I might have been able to guess something."

He stared at her, bewildered.

"Guess something?"

"Didn't you ever find the thought crossing your mind?"

"What thought?"

"That she liked him."

"Liked him?"

"Oh George, haven't you realized who it is?"

"I can't very well realize who it is until you tell me who it is, can I?"

"Paul Merrion."

"Merrion? Look here, Eunice, you'd better read that letter again; you're all mixed up. Merrion's engaged to be married."

"But George, that was over and—"

"She told me herself, first day she arrived. He brought her up from the station and they got out my drink and toasted the—"

"It was broken off. It was over months ago."

"Nobody told me anything about any breaking-off."

"It's off, all the same. And Lydia's going to marry him, and she wants to know if you'll give her away. You will, won't you?"

"Paul Merrion!"

"You're pleased, aren't you? I do hope so, George. I know this must be a surprise, but—"

He had ceased to lean on the hoe; he was standing upright.

"Surprise? Who said it was a surprise?" he demanded.

"Well . . . isn't it? Unless you guessed when—"

"I don't think you've realized that I've always taken a fatherly interest in all four girls, but especially in Lydia. Surprise? Why did she come to Ellstream in May? I'll tell you. She came because I'm a far-seeing man, and I thought it might be as well to get her down here while that fellow was here."

"Paul Merrion?"

"Certainly. If you feel that two young people would make a suitable pair, how can they pair up if you don't

225

throw them together? So I suggested her coming here. If you don't believe me, ask your sister. She'll confirm that I went over to see Mrs. Merrion, had a chat with this young chap, and came home with my mind made up. It was just a chance, of course—but it's paid off, hasn't it?"

"You mean you ... actually ... Oh George, I would never have believed that you would ..."

"It was time she got herself a husband. I simply did my bit to help her, that's all. Put her in the way of someone who'd look after her ..."

An exchange of a different kind was taking place near the riding school at St. Godric's. Yolanda, after a prolonged search, had run down her quarry.

"Have you got a minute, Dudley? I—"

"No. Sorry."

"Then just half a minute. I've had the most wonderful idea for the wedding."

"Wedding?"

"Paul and Lydia's. I was thinking what a pity it was that they wouldn't be able to come out of the church under an archway of swords, and suddenly I had this idea. I want to get some of the boys from the riding school and line them up in a double row outside the church and they can—"

"—hold up their swords?"

"Not swords, silly. Their riding crops."

"Are you completely crazy?"

"What's crazy about that?"

"Do you think the bridal couple could walk upright under an arch made by pygmies?"

"I could choose the tallest boys and—"

"No."

"You don't like the idea?"

"No."

"But—"

"I said No. Absolutely and finally No."

"Oh well, I suppose you know best."

"Yes. Always. Remember that."

If Mr. Ainstey's claim to have engineered the engagement was somewhat unfounded, there was no doubt about his making himself felt in the course of the preparations for the wedding. The first decision made by Paul and Lydia—a quiet wedding with nobody present but the immediate family—he brushed aside. The wedding would take place in Ellstream. And from his house. The offer made by Lady Charlotte to hold the reception in her house, he refused even to discuss; he would not, he stated, set foot over her threshold. If they wanted to have the wedding there, let them, but rule him out.

The date of the wedding was for some time a difficulty. There was no hurry, the couple reiterated. Christmas, perhaps.

But before Christmas, cold descended upon the land and found its way into the little apartment in which Paul had spent so many happy leisure hours. He had made it, for a time, a refuge, a hiding place in which he and Lydia passed what they would one day recall as one of the happiest periods of their life together. They were content; they met when their work was over, they saw the shortening evenings closing round their windows; they wanted nobody but one another. Until the frosts came, and Paul put a question.

"What do you do for heating in the winter?"

"Well, there aren't any fireplaces, and I hate oil stoves, and . . . well, I put on extra sweaters."

He shivered.

"And boots, and mittens and mufflers," he supplemented. "This place is for summer living." He lifted one of her hands and began to count the fingers. "This little pig," he said, pausing at the third, "will shortly have a wedding ring on it."

"I've been happy here."

"So have I—up to now. But there's a certain lack of comfort; my toes keep freezing. We're going to look for a house with allover heating, and you'll be able to take off your extra sweaters and I'll see to it that you're warm, day and night. For ever and ever, in fact. Say after me: Paul, I love you very much."

"Paul, I love you. Very, very much."

It was the most picturesque wedding—and the most fashionable—that Ellstream had ever known or was likely to know. Mrs. Merrion's pleas that none of her old friends and acquaintances should be hurt by being left out, ensured that almost the entire population of the town attended the ceremony. The reception was in a hall in the town, bare and austere before Mrs. Merrion and her assistants had transformed it. Lady Charlotte was at the church, but to the relief of everybody pleaded fatigue and did not attend the reception.

Two small packages were delivered by the postman on the day before the wedding. The recipients were Lydia and Mrs. Merrion; the contents were two diamond brooches. There was no card and no message; the postmark was Fez. To Mrs. Merrion's amazed speculation as to how, when and where Esmond had fallen on his feet, Paul and Lydia offered no comment. The game had been played, and Esmond had won.

THE DANGER

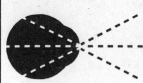

This Large Print Book carries the
Seal of Approval of N.A.V.H.